Lizzie's Tale

Old Balmain House Series
Book 2

Graham Wilson

BOOKS BY THIS AUTHOR

Children of Arnhem's Kaleidoscope – A Memoir

Old Balmain House Series
  Little Lost Girl – Book 1
  Lizzie's Tale   – Book 2
  Devil's Choice – Book 3

Crocodile Spirit Dreaming Series
Just Visiting   – Book 1
Creature of an Ancient Dreaming   – Book 2
The Empty Place   – Book 3
Lost Girls   – Book 4
Sunlit Shadow Dance   – Book 5

READER REVIEWS OF OLD BALMAIN HOUSE SERIES

Amazon Reviews

★★★★★ Great Read

This is the story of three houses and the people who built them and lived in them from the mid-1800s to the present day. Told in a rather quaint and old-fashioned manner, it is a wonderful portrayal of a multi-generational family who lived through good times and bad, but always retained a strong family bond. The growth of this area seen through their eyes is fascinating. And, the mystery of Sophie's disappearance is enough to keep one reading

★★★★★ Wonderful books

I'm so glad I got all these books in a set. Each book reached further into the story, always going forward, but also bringing the past as the story unfolded. Well-written characters, and such detail that I felt I was walking alongside them as I read. No imagination is needed to see the people and places in your mind. Vivid descriptions brought the time and place to mind easily. Kindle said it would take more than 9 hours to read it. I did it over two days...I could not put it down! I've always dreamed of visiting Australia, and these books just increased that dream. Well worth reading!!!

★★★★★ Absolutely loved this series

Absolutely loved this series. I could not put it down, it has held me riveted to each story and looking for more. I could vividly imagine each tale and description of the places even though I haven't been there. I would recommend this collection to anyone who wants to read about the settlers in Australia passing through generations and the fast paced tale that goes with all the books in the collection. Well Done Graham Wilson. Can't wait to read the Crocodile Spirit Dreaming books now I have purchased them.

★★★★ Really enjoyed this story

Really enjoyed this story. Not so much historical Australian fiction out there. Made me go looking up the area online to see where they were talking about. It was sad and moved a bit quick through the characters at times but I thought it recreated the time period really well. Hard to imagine Sydney with that few people.

★★★★★ Five Stars

A brilliant read, very interesting

Barnes and Noble Reviews

***** **I absolutely loved both stories**
I highly recommend you get to read. Definitely looking forward to reading more by this author. Awesome!!!! Held my attention to the very end

***** **A truly inspiring story, brought teams to my eyes**

***** **Wonderful**
A beautiful story that will stay with me. Loved it and wanted it to continue. One of the best I have read lately.

***** **Lizzy's story**
An amazing story, couldn't put it down. The author has written one of the best books I have read of this type. I was critical of the series he wrote at first but he had grown to be a favourite of mine. A dramatic, fast paced, loving and exciting story.

***** **If I could give it 6 stars I would!!!**
It is not often a book will bring actual tears to my eyes but this one did as well as kept me up well past bedtime. If it does not touch you similarly I would be very surprised!!!

Kobo Reviews

***** **Old Balmain House Book Series**
Wonderful I couldn't bear to put them down.......wishing there were more in the series. The people were so real it's almost like I've met them.

***** **Lizzies's tale**
If we all had just some of Lizzies courage our world would be a much better place to live in. Such a nice story so interesting. Great read

***** **A moving delight**
A great story about a courageous young girl who triumphs despite adversity. The world needs more stories like this.

ACKNOWLEDGMENTS

Many people have reviewed this novel in the four years since it was first published. Your advice, mostly positive, is greatly valued.

THANK YOU ALL.

From reader reviews and a structural review by KJ Eyre, I have substantially revised this book and released a new edition It has many changes but keeps the main elements of the original story. The house and Sydney location are important parts of the background, which give context and place the story. Hence the 'Old Balmain House Series' name keeps this sense of location within the story.

The cover for this second edition has been produced by Nada Backovic. I thank her for her creative flair in taking my description of story elements and creating an outstanding image which captures part of the essence of this story. Arcangel Images supplied the background image for this cover.

Part of the inspiration for this book and series came from reading Geraldine Brooks novel, 'People of the Book', which used small artefacts of history to carry people's stories from the past into the present day.

Contents

Authors Preface

This novel continues the Old Balmain House Series. It begins in the same house as the first book. It tells of a poor family who live here at a time when Australia was moving into the 1960s; a highly conservative society, but on the brink of major change.

It centres around the life of a girl who makes a painful journey from childhood to adulthood, at a time when unmarried teenage pregnancy almost invariably meant forced adoption and when the social stigma for unwed mothers made their lives unbelievably difficult.

While the characters are not based on real people, the treatment of pregnant women in this society and, in particular, the consequences for teenage girls who became pregnant outside marriage, were real features of Australian life in the 1960s. Therefore this story is something that could have happened to a person like my imagined character, Lizzie; so it becomes her tale.

Some people have told me that someone of Lizzie's age could not have done the things she did in this book, that there was no way she could have displayed this level of maturity. However 100 years earlier girls of this age regularly got married, had babies and fulfilled their parental responsibilities from their mid-teens. It was a matter of necessity in these times.

My experience of Australian life in the 1960's and 1970's, particularly in small towns, is these were very trusting places, people were accepted at face value, identity documents were rarely required and, provided they met society's behaviour expectations, people got on with their lives with minimal interference from others.

I also have no doubt people can act with a maturity well beyond then years when needs require. So I think the story of Lizzie as a fifteen and sixteen year old remains realistic. It seems that many of my readers, particularly those of older generations, concur with this view!

Prologue

It was September 1956, a warm spring morning in Sydney. Lizzie lay in her bed, she loved her room. It looked out onto the Smith Street, Balmain. In the early morning the sunshine came in, helping her get up for school.

Lizzie would turn eight soon and felt very proud to be able to walk up to school on her own. She did not have any brothers and sisters, though her parents kept trying to have more children. But she did not care; she was happy, really happy. She had the most wonderful friend, a friend named Sophie.

Sophie was just eight too. She lived in their chimney; that is what Sophie told her. She had seen Sophie lots of times, mostly after the lights were turned out. Sophie always wore a school dress. She told Lizzie she went to the same school as Lizzie did. But Lizzie had never seen Sophie at school, and Sophie's uniform did not look like hers; it looked oldish, longer and sort of quaint, like the clothes you saw in photos taken before the war.

The only trouble was that nobody else believed that Sophie was real. Lizzie had told her Mum and Dad about Sophie. They listened politely but she knew they did not believe her. Later she had heard her Mum say that Sophie was Lizzie's imaginary friend.

But Sophie was real; really real. They told stories together for hours and Sophie knew things that only real people could possibly know. She had told Lizzie of a special place in the school yard where she, with her own friend Matty, hid a jar with coloured stones and carved wood toys. Lizzie had found it, just where Sophie had said it would be. Sophie said Lizzie could keep these thing; they were hers to give away. Lizzie was delighted even though they looked a bit old fashioned too. So she hid them in her bottom drawer; she did not want other people to see them and laugh.

Yesterday Lizzie had done a job for Sophie, an important job. Sophie had told Lizzie her own Mum, Maria, was old and sick and asked Lizzie to go and visit her. Sophie said her Mum was really missing her and her Dad, Jimmy, who was now staying with her. Sophie she said she wanted her Mum to know that she and her Dad were together again, were both happy and could not wait until her Mum came to see them too. Then they would all be happy together. Sophie had asked Lizzie to go and tell her Mum, Maria, this as soon as she could.

So, yesterday, after school, Lizzie had followed Sophie's directions and walked to a big house in East Balmain, a house Sophie said was her grandmother's house. It was a long way, but Lizzie did not mind, she knew it was really important. When she got there, she banged on the door for a long time. Finally a lady, a nurse who said her name was 'Sister Rebecca', came to the door.

Lizzie told Sister Rebecca that she wanted to see Mrs Maria because she had a message from Sophie. At first the nurse told her to stop being silly and go away. But Mrs Maria must have heard Lizzie because she called out and asked who it was.

She heard the nurse say "It's just a silly school girl called Lizzie. She says she wants to tell you a message from Sophie.

Straightaway Lizzie was called into this lady's room. The lady asked the nurse to go away and close the door. The nurse did, even though she grumbled out loud.

Then the lady asked her to come and sit on the bed, right next to her. The lady was very old and thin. But she had the most beautiful eyes; and when Lizzie looked at them she felt like she was talking to Sophie. On the dresser beside her bed was a picture of Sophie, the same as now, except in the picture she was wearing a white dress. There was also a picture of this lady, when she was young and beautiful; standing next to a man who was Sophie's Daddy, Jimmy. Somehow Lizzie knew it was him in their wedding photo.

Lizzie told her Sophie's message. At first the lady sat very still for a long minute, then she cried, but they were happy tears. Then the lady told her, if she saw Sophie again, to say to Sophie she was already packing her bags and hoped to come that night.

Last night, after this, Lizzie had seen Sophie again. Lizzie thought it might be the last time she would see Sophie like an ordinary person. Sophie was starting to fade away; Lizzie could look through her now and see across the room. Sophie had been so happy. She had told Lizzie that, even though they would not see each other after this, they would stay best, best friends, for ever and ever, and Lizzie could still talk to her and that she would hear and understand.

So, although Sophie was gone and Lizzie could no longer see her, she knew they would stay friends. This made her feel good. She knew she did not need to feel lonely, as Sophie would keep listening to her. So she smiled a happy smile as she lay in her bed in the morning sun.

That day, after school finished, Lizzie saw Mrs Maria's photo in the newspaper. The paper said that Mrs Maria Williams of East Balmain had died last night. Lizzie felt sad about this but it made sense; when Mrs Maria said she was packing up to leave what she really meant was she was dying.

Lizzie had begun to understand this when Sophie faded away last night. Then she realised that, while Sophie was real, she was also a ghost of someone who had lived before and died a long time ago, at the time when Mrs Maria was young herself. That was why nobody else could see her. Now Sophie did not need Lizzie's help anymore. She had gone to another place with her own Mum and Dad, a place where no one living now could see her. Lizzie knew it was a happy place, because she could feel the happiness in Sophie. Perhaps it was that place grown-ups called heaven, which they talked about in church.

Just before she had left Mrs Maria's place, yesterday, Mrs Maria had given Lizzie a small package wrapped in plain brown paper. It fitted into the palm of Lizzie's hand. Mrs Maria said it was a present for her from Sophie, it was a present that Sophie's grandmother Alison, had given Sophie when she turned six and it was special because it had a little bit of magic in it, magic just for Lizzie.

Mrs Maria said that Lizzie should not open it unless a time came when she really, really needed it. In the meantime she should put it somewhere safe, but she must take it with her if ever she moved to another place to live.

So Lizzie made a solemn promise that she would never open it, unless she really needed help. She knew she would keep this promise. For now she put it into the purse which she had been given as a present on her last birthday. To make sure it did not fall out she cut a little slit into the lining and put it inside the lining material before sewing the lining up again. This was the best and safest place she could think of, a place where no one else would know but where she could take it out again if she needed to.

Chapter 1 - The Dream - 1963

Lizzie found herself lying awake in her bed. At first she found it hard to tell whether she was awake or asleep. She knew she had been dreaming and the dream still felt so incredibly real. But now she looked through the window and saw the familiar outline of the tree in the faded street light. So she knew it was definitely her bedroom window not some imaginary place in her mind.

This was the most vivid dream she could ever remember having and it was a scary dream in which Sophie had tried to tell her something. It was a dream of warning, though the warning was hard to understand. The first part she could remember was that she was in a car with some boys. The boys were a few years older than her. She was with Julie, her best friend, and they were going to a party.

They were all dressed up and excited. Julie was even more striking and elegant than normal with her shoulder length fair hair, lipstick and eye shadow. And Lizzie felt really pretty too, Julie had styled her short dark hair into a fashionable bob and made up her face with rich red lipstick and mascara that made her dark eyes stand out and gave her a sophisticated look. She wore a lemon coloured dress of a soft flowing material. It must be Julie's; it was far more glamourous than anything she owned. It had shoes to match with heels which made her look tall.

One of the men seemed to be Julie's boyfriend, they were holding hands together. The others were people she did not know, but they must have been rich because one of them owned the car they were riding in, and they were all well dressed with expensive clothes.

Later in the dream, three of these boys wanted her to leave the party and come for a drive with them. Julie and her boyfriend were still at the party talking to some other people and she could not really see them. Lizzie sort of liked the boy who owned the car and he seemed to like her. Now he wanted her to come back to the car with him.

As Lizzie stood outside the front door of the party house, deciding whether to go, suddenly, there was Sophie standing in front of her.

Sophie was pulling at her arm and trying to get her to go back inside. Sophie was just the same as she had looked all those years ago, when she had lived in her bedroom chimney. Now she seemed so little; quite babyish really. She stood right in front of Lizzie, trying to block her from going to the car with her boys, saying it was dangerous. She begged Lizzie not to go.

But Lizzie had walked straight through where Sophie was standing. It felt like she was knocking Sophie aside, even though she disappeared before Lizzie got there. Of course Sophie was not really there. Now Lizzie was awake she realised that it was only a dream, even though it felt real. Sophie was only ever a ghost and she vanished from Lizzie's life a long time ago, when Lizzie was only seven or eight. She could not remember talking to Sophie since when her Dad was living here. So she decided it would be childish to listen to her now.

Soon Lizzie would be fifteen. It was silly to let something from all those years ago interfere with her life now. Sure she had promised Sophie they would stay best friends for ever, but that was just a kid promise; one did not pay attention to those when grown up, as she was now.

But, as she tried to brush this dream aside, she had a bad feeling. A voice inside her head kept telling her that she must listen to Sophie, that Sophie was her real friend and would not come all the way to tell her this thing unless it really mattered.

The trouble was that neither she nor Julie had a boyfriend. Certainly they knew no one like the boys in the dream. And, even if they did and went for a ride in a car with these boys, what harm could it do. Deciding that she had thought about it enough she fell back to sleep. When she woke in the morning the dream was pushed out of her mind, soon to be almost forgotten.

It did come back, just for a second, when she saw Julie. But it seemed too silly to tell her grown up and fashionable friend, the one everyone in school had voted the cleverest, most beautiful and most likely to succeed person. If the truth was told Lizzie was in awe of Julie who seemed much cleverer and prettier than she was, with her blond hair and perfect features. Julie had much nicer clothes and other good things because her parents had a lot more money. She lived in a big house over near Birchgrove Oval, and her Dad worked in an office in the city and drove a fancy car called a Jaguar. Perhaps Julie did know real boys like the ones in her dream, but she had never introduced people like them to Lizzie.

Despite their different lives Julie had become her friend at school and most morning teas and lunchtimes they sat together and talked to each other. Lizzie did not know why Julie payed attention to her. Even though boys at school seemed to like Lizzie too she realised she was much plainer than her beautiful friend and her clothes and hair were not nearly as nice. She made her own clothes with her mother's sewing machine using whatever material was available. Julie bought hers in expensive department stores, places like David Jones in Elizabeth Street.

Lizzie was fourteen and would be fifteen soon. She had lived in the same house and slept in the same bed for all the life she could remember. But much had changed from the life of her childhood.

Lizzie now had one brother, David. He was six years old. Her Mum had three miscarriages, after she was born before David came along. After each of these her mother seemed to go off to a place inside herself where she barely talked to other people and forgot to do all those things that ordinary people did, things like housework, going shopping, or putting on nice clothes. Sometimes, for days at a time, her mother would barely come out of her room, and she would forget to wash herself, do her hair or almost anything. Then it was just Lizzie and her Dad, Ronnie to her Mum, who had to manage. Lizzie started to do housework and cooking, even though she could not do it as well as her Mum.

At first her Dad had been good and had tried to get her Mum out. He had also helped to do a lot of the housework. But as it went on, year after year, gradually it began to get her Dad down too. He always worked long days on the docks and it was hard heavy work, lifting and carting things. So he would come home tired and dirty. However when Lizzie was little he always came straight home and would pick her up and swing her around in his arms and hug her. And he would hug his wife, Patsy, and dance her around the room to make her laugh.

The first miscarriage came when Lizzie was about five or six and she could only kind of remember it. She knew that the baby had been born way too soon; it was only about four months old. Her Dad had said it was as tiny as a little finger. This first time her Dad had tried really hard to get her Mum to come out and keep doing things. He had helped heaps, and their family life had still been good. He told her Mum they needed to keep trying and he was sure they would have another baby soon.

Sure enough, soon, maybe a few months later, another baby came, but this one was also lost around four or five months. Her Mum had sparked up while the baby was coming but, all too soon, it was over and she was back to being miserable again.

Her Dad kept trying to help and Lizzie tried really hard to help too, and their Mum seemed to appreciate they were both trying. She stayed upbeat about her chance to have another baby and said that this time it would come out alright. It was like she made this promise to them and herself that it would work out right this time, a sort of bargain.

After another year or two, when Lizzie was around seven, her Mum got pregnant again. She had become her old self again, talking, laughing and playing with Lizzie, going out with her friends, going to the shops to buy baby clothes for the boy she was sure it was. And her Dad seemed really excited and happy too. All the pregnancy it seemed to go just fine and, gradually, her Mum's tummy got bigger and bigger.

But then, when it came time for the baby to be born, it all went horribly wrong. The baby was turned the wrong way, and the cord got twisted around its neck. Her Mum was rushed up to the hospital where they did an operation. They cut her tummy open and took the baby out. But the baby was dead; this little blue thing, which should have been her new brother Ronnie.

For a while her Mum had tried to be brave. That was the year she turned eight, the last happy year Lizzie could remember. Her mother kept saying that soon another baby would come. But it seemed like the operation had messed up something in her insides, she would often hold her stomach in pain. Gradually she started not getting up in the morning and doing less and less. Now Lizzie found herself doing more and more around the house to help her Mum again.

It would not have been too bad if her Mum had been pleased with Lizzie's help; but instead she found fault with whatever was done, the meals were not nice, the clothes were not washed properly, the floors were dirty; that's what she said while she lay around, doing nothing.

She acted the same way towards her Dad too. He could not do a single thing right. On the one hand she said he did not work hard enough and earn enough money. On the other hand she said it was his fault that he worked such long hours and came home late. Lizzie knew it was unfair to both her Dad and her; they were both trying their best. But she could not make her Mum understand. Gradually they both stopped trying to please her and started to ignore her and leave her to herself.

Her Dad started stopping at the pub on the way home and often spent most of his wages there. Lizzie would take any chance to go to a friend's place and not come home till late and when she did come home now she would often sit in her room and read books, just to escape this poor and dreary life. She kept trying her best to look after her Dad, but it was hard now when he was often drunk. It also seemed that every time her Mum and Dad were together they either fought or had nothing to do with each other and this made her Dad miserable and grumpy.

Lizzie had really wanted to have her old happy life back, just her with her Mum and Dad, all being happy together. She could not really see why having another baby was so important to them. Sure it would be nice for her to have a brother, but they were still a family and could enjoy things.

Then, just when it had seemed hopeless, her Mum had come out of the bedroom one day with her hair washed and wearing clean clothes. She told them she was expecting another baby. After this it was like she had become a new person, she cleaned the house until it was spotless, she made them keep everything really clean; she said she was not going to let anything happen this time which might put at risk this precious child. Everything was about the baby that was coming, nothing about anyone else. It felt as if her Mum had forgotten about her Dad and her, even though they were still living here too.

Soon her Dad was going back to the pub again, coming home late, drunk, having spent far too much money. Her Mum could not stand this either. Before long she would not let him stop in the same room as her, she said he was too dirty. Her Dad would still hug her, his Lizzie, when he saw her and she hugged him back tightly. Even though he had often not shaved and smelt a bit bad, she still loved him lots. She just wished she could make it all better.

Then one day he did not come home. He was not there that night and not the next night either. Lizzie was beside herself with worry, even if her Mum barely seemed to notice. Her tummy was getting really big now, and all she seemed to talk about was what would be good for the baby. It was as if her husband's absence barely registered in her mind.

So Lizzie went to the place where her Dad worked, early the next morning, and asked if he was there. The people said that no-one had seen him since the night before last when he finished work. He had told them he was finished for the day, obviously heading for the pub.

So she had gone to the pub, just herself, an eight year old girl in a school dress, even though she should have gone to school. She asked if anyone had seen her Dad or knew where he was. Finally someone told her he had been there the night before last and had left about ten o'clock, so drunk he could barely walk, saying there was no point going home as his wife did not talk to him anymore, as he wobbled out the door.

That was the last anyone had seen him. The publican said that, if he had gone missing, Lizzie should go and see the police. So she had walked all the way up to the police station, up in the middle of town, and talked to a kindly police sergeant. She had asked him to help her look for her Dad and had also told him about her Mum and how her Mum did not seem to realise her that Dad was missing.

So the policeman organised a search with a few men from the pub and from the nearby streets. They found him soon enough, lying at the bottom of some rickety stairs which went down from behind the pub; going down the side of the cliffs to the docks below. Underneath the stairs grew some scrubby bushes.

There was the body of her Dad, lying hidden under these bushes. They said he must have tripped and fallen over the rails, coming from high up on the stairs, falling headfirst onto the rocky ground below. Now he lay there with his head smashed and his neck at a funny angle. It was awful.

They tried to keep her away; they said he smelt bad and she should not see him until the undertaker had fixed him up. But she had ducked under peoples arms and ran to where he was; just wanting to go and hug him one more time. A policeman caught her and held her back, but not before she saw him with his broken neck and smashed head.

Since then she could not quite forgive her Mum for letting this happen, through sending her father away. She knew it was not just her Mum's fault; but if her Mum had been nicer her Dad would not have got so drunk and it would not have happened.

Now six more years had gone by. Her Mum had baby David soon after this. While Lizzie quite liked her brother, she could not get the thing she most wanted, to have her Dad back. So now, while her Mum tried to talk to Lizzie again and pretend as if it had not happened, Lizzie was angry deep inside. Even though they still lived together and she played a bit with her brother, she mostly kept to herself.

And now they were so, so poor. Her mother got some sort of pension, but it did not go far towards feeding them and buying clothes. The house needed a new coat of paint, the kitchen cupboards were falling apart and there were holes in the bottom of her shoes that she tried to stuff with newspaper.

She looked for any odd jobs she could find; baby-sitting, mending clothes, washing and ironing, running errands; but it was always hard to earn enough money and what she got she gave straight to her Mum without keeping any for herself, because she knew that her family was more important and her Dad would have wanted her to do this.

She knew her Mum was trying to make it up to her for that awful time she had caused, but yet in Lizzie's heart a hard lump towards her Mum remained, like a piece of ice or stone.

But, at last, things were looking up, Julie had become her good friend and Julie was rich and had other rich friends. Julie talked to Lizzie like she was not some little poor girl and, sometimes, she gave her spare clothes, bits of jewellery and other nice things. Plus she really liked talking to Julie, with both of them telling stories and imagining what they would do with their lives once grown up. Soon she would leave school; it would happen at the end of this year as she had been promised work in a factory in Pyrmont. She was not sure what the job was but the pay was a pound a day which seemed a huge sum, and the money would really help her family. Now she was determined to forget about any silly dreams like the one last night.

Chapter 2 – Lizzie Turns Fifteen

The year was 1963 and soon it would be in 1964. It was the last week of school at Balmain High School. Lizzie and Julie had sat their final exam for their Intermediate Certificate. Lizzie generally got good marks, people said she was bright and should stay on at school. Julie was going to Croydon Presbyterian Ladies College next year as a boarder, Lizzie's Mum said it was a sort of finishing school for rich girls, before they went and found husbands and got married.

Julie however had other ideas and talked about going to University and doing some course, perhaps Arts or becoming a lawyer. She was bright and got good marks too, but usually Lizzie beat her in this, at least in Maths and Science. Julie really encouraged Lizzie to not leave school; she said she was way too clever to end up working in a factory, packing boxes or something similar.

But there was not enough money in their family for that, her Mum was barely managing to make ends meet. Lizzie knew it was time for her to get a job and contribute to the family income. Now a job was on offer in Pyrmont and she would start it in two weeks.

Right now she had two more days to go at school. Then, on Saturday, it was her birthday party; she would turn fifteen. She knew her Mum had been scrimping and saving every little bit she could in order to have enough money to give her a nice party where she could invite a few school friends. She even suspected that her Mum was trying to buy her a present from David Jones on lay by, she saw what looked like a lay by docket in her Mum's purse the other day.

She and her Mum were getting on better now; she was starting to appreciate just how hard it was for her Mum to bring up two children on her own. Her Mum had no other family that lived in Sydney, her own mother and father were both dead and her one brother lived in Melbourne. While he wrote occasional letters he did not have a good enough job to help with money. And since her husband, Ron's, death, her Mum had heard nothing from his family. It was as if they blamed

Patsy for Ron's death. While Lizzie knew this was part true, she was last managing to forgive and forget, and she thought they should too.

Lizzie had also read about a thing called post-natal depression that doctors were talking about, she read lots of science books and had started to understand it was a sort of mental illness. She thought that this was what her mother had before and that it was not fair to blame people in this situation. So, even though she still missed her Dad terribly, that hard lump in her heart towards her Mum was slowly going away.

Lizzie knew she was not exactly beautiful. People told her she had a bright, interesting face and, in the last year, her body had filled out, although she did not have the radiant beauty of Julie. But people seemed to enjoy talking to her and thought she had interesting things to say. She had lots of ideas in school discussions and her teachers were all most encouraging for her to try and continue her studies.

The day of Lizzie's birthday came around; it was a Saturday, and her Mum had organised an afternoon party, starting at three o'clock in their back yard. This was shaded by a big gum tree, and her mother had set up a table for food, surrounded by all the chairs she owned, along with as many more as she could borrow from neighbours, arranged in little clusters in the leafy garden. Her Mum had always been a really talented cook; she had worked in a hotel preparing food for a couple years before she met Lizzie's Dad and got married. Today it seemed that she had excelled herself, everything she had prepared looked and smelt delicious. David had been given the job of decorating it all using ribbons, balloons and streamers. He had taken to this with gusto; now it had a really festive air.

Six of Lizzie's classmates were coming, including Julie, along with two other friends around Lizzie's age who lived in her street. The neighbours from both sides, who had helped with the cooking and preparing food, were also coming.

Julie had also asked if she could bring a friend of her own, someone Lizzie did not know. The way she said it, it sounded sort of significant and it made her wonder if Julie had started seeing someone.

Just before three o'clock the neighbours came round; they offered to help with any last minute arrangements. The Locke family were a young couple, with a boy around David's age, who lived to their right. The two boys immediately disappeared into David's attic bedroom, not expected to come out again until the food was served.

Mr and Mrs Collins, who lived on the other side, were an elderly couple whose children had grown up and moved away. They were kind, if a little nosey. However their help was welcome, even if they were too churchy for Lizzie's taste. Lizzie greeted them politely and chatted with them for a minute to be courteous while her mother worked away. Then Mr Collins took up the role of serving drinks to other guests and Mrs Collins took up the job of keeping an eye on the pies and cakes which were finishing in the oven while her Mum attended to other arrangements.

Today Lizzie felt inordinately proud of her Mum. Sure their house looked old and shabby. But her Mum had done everything humanly possible to make it look its best, it was spotless and bunches of flowers graced all possible locations. And she was amazed with the food her Mum had put together, little pies and pastries, sweet cakes, some bread, cold meat, cheese and fruit and lots of lollies and chocolates. It looked beyond wonderful.

The door bell rang. It was five of her classmates, come together, each with their own present, bright wrapping and brighter smiles. It was lovely and so exciting that these people had brought these things for her.

A big car drove past and parked just in front of the next house. Lizzie barely looked at it, none of her friends owned cars. Then a noise drew her eyes that way and she noticed Julie sitting in the passenger seat, wearing a lilac summer dress and looking gorgeous. And there was a tall, good looking man sitting in the driver's seat. He got out, came around to Julie's side and courteously opened the door. Julie got out, trying to look grown up and graceful, but obviously a bit self-conscious. The man took her hand and they walked together up to the front door, where Julie introduced Lizzie, sounding formal. "Lizzie, this is my friend Carl who I wanted you to meet." "Carl, this is my best friend from school, Lizzie."

Julie handed her a beautifully wrapped present, along with a card. Lizzie brought all her guests into the house and introduced them all around. The party began, everyone chatting politely and sipping punch; then presents were given which Lizzie dutifully opened. Julie had given her a lovely embroidered top and a swim suit with the fashion house label still attached. Her other friends had given her a range of other considerate gifts, for all of which she dutifully showed enthusiasm.

Last was a present from her Mum, the soft shape showed it was clothing. She opened it; it was a stunning summer dress, beautiful floral patterns and soft silky fabric. She knew this would have cost her Mum big time, scrimping and saving for months and then some. She could feel tears prick her eyes, and her Mum seemed to be crying too.

Her Mum said. "Lizzie, I only wish your Dad could have been here to see you in it, I know he would have approved and been so proud."

Lizzie went over and hugged her Mum. It was like all the hate and badness of the years was finally washed away.

Chapter 3 - The Party

On Monday next week Julie called round to Lizzie's place about lunch time. Lizzie was just hanging about, feeling at a loose end. So it was a relief to have a chance to chat to Julie. With all the other people their chance to talk at the party had been limited. So they walked around the corner to the park where they sat under a shady tree to talk in private without disturbance.

Lizzie was bursting to know more about Carl; she wanted to know how and when Julie met him, how serious it was, what they had done together and so many more things. She had never had a boyfriend herself and part of her was jealous. There was so little time, so much work to be done and she was not striking to look at, at least not the way Julie was. Not to mention that her clothes were often threadbare, her Mum cut her hair in a simple plain manner, and she had not practised all the ways of making herself attractive to men that most of her other friends had.

She knew a couple other boys around her age in her street but the relationship was like brothers and sisters, they had never taken any particular notice of her and she had never taken any real notice of them. But she sensed that there were other boys out there who were different creatures, charming and sophisticated, like those she had read about in the great novels of English which she studied at school and read in her bedroom at home.

Carl seemed like one of these sophisticated boys, resembling a figure from a novel, who dressed in striking clothes, drove a luxurious car and who knew how to laugh and make jokes in ways which charmed girls. So she had a hunger to know about him, and other men like him, who mixed with the likes of Julie, and bombarded her with questions, 'Tell me where you met him, tell me what he does, have you ever kissed him?" Her questions went on and on.

Julie basked in Lizzie's enthusiastic excitement; "Yes, he is handsome; yes, he has a lot of other friends who are like him."

Julie told Lizzie she had met Carl at a party that she had gone to with her parents, at a family friend's house in Woollahra, a couple weeks before their exams. He was nineteen and working in an office in the city, which was part of a business owned by his father. He had invited her to come to the movies with him the day after they met. Her parents had given a guarded OK; yes, but she needed to be home an hour after the movie finished.

Carl had complied with this direction like the perfect gentleman. He had taken her hand during the movie and had given her a kiss on the cheek when he said goodnight. And riding with him in the car was great fun. After that they arranged to meet the following weekend when he had invited her to come to the beach with him for the afternoon, saying that he was going with his parents and some other friends. Of his parents there was no sign but she had met some other boys and a couple other girls who seemed to hang out with them. They had all gone swimming together in the sea at Manly and at one stage Carl had picked her up and kissed her on the lips, and she kind of liked it, it gave her a funny feeling in that place.

He had not tried to do any more but she could tell he was attracted to her and she knew that more would come soon if they kept going out, he had hinted at that. While she knew she had to be careful she was kind of interested herself to try some more kissing and whatever followed, not going all the way of course, but plenty was exciting to try before then.

Julie and Lizzie talked wonderingly about what it would be like to go all the way. For both of them it had little more meaning than some imaginary pleasure, talked about in books and glimpsed in movies. Neither of their parents ever talked about this with them, but they had the general idea from biology and other books, if not the exact details.

Julie told her she had started to tell fibs to her parents about going out with Carl, she had not let on that Carl's parents were not there on the beach that day. And now they had arranged to meet at the beach again tomorrow. Julie had told her Mum and Dad that she was going shopping in the city with a couple of other girls, when actually she was going to catch the ferry over to Manly to meet Carl and his friends for another day at the beach.

Julie said, "I am kind of hoping you could come with me, wear your new bathing suit, the boys are sure to think you look good in that. But you must not tell anyone else about it or, you know how gossip gets around, next thing the story will get back to my parents. Then I will be grounded."

Lizzie felt a tingle of excitement at the thought of this adventure. Of course she would come, she would catch the bus into the city, saying she was meeting Julie there, to give Julie her opinion of some clothes and other things that Julie wanted to buy, and that they would not be back until late, as they would go to a movie while they were there.

Next day they met in the mid-morning at Circular Quay. Julie bought them both an ice-cream and handed Lizzie a ferry ticket which she had bought for her. Lizzie felt embarrassed at taking things from Julie, but Julie said not to be silly, her parents were rich and they gave her plenty of pocket money, more than enough for them both to share. So Lizzie accepted.

It was really exciting on the ferry, Lizzie could only remember going once before, with her Mum and Dad when she was little. Now she felt so grown up as the two of them stood by the rail with the breeze blowing in their hair and chatted. She noticed that several young men were paying attention to them as if they were suddenly beautiful, but then she thought, *Well, of course, it's Julie, men and boys always notice her.*

At Manly they walked along the Corso until they came to the beach, where Julie pointed out her friends lying together in a group on the sand. Some of the boys looked very grown up and muscular, the other girls also looked grown up, wearing swimmers that really showed off their bodies.

Lizzie realised that she was lucky to have a new swim suit as the old one was much too small and raggy; it did not fit her body properly anymore, looked sort of babyish, and the material was faded and fraying. But she felt self-conscious showing so much of herself to these almost total strangers in her new bathing suit. Carl was the only one she had met before and she had barely said hello to him. So, for a while, she left her shirt top on to keep hiding her body which was very obvious in the swimmers. But then, feeling like a party pooper, she removed her shirt and lay out on the sand, sunning herself in her swimmers, just like the others were doing.

All the friends seemed nice. There were six men aged from eighteen to twenty and two other girls as well as her and Julie. One said she was sixteen though, when Lizzie looked closely at her, she seemed no older than Lizzie was, and the other was seventeen. Julie went and sat with Carl and the two of them were holding hands. The other girls each seemed to each be with one of the boys. So that left three of the boys who seemed to all want to talk to Lizzie and entertain her. This made Lizzie feel very flattered, particularly when they all told her things like how good she looked in her swimsuit and what beautiful hair she had.

Their leader was a big strong looking boy named Martin. He said he had come down from Newcastle last year, along with his other two friends, Dan and Will. Dan and Will seemed like his followers, rather than other men out for their own good time, laughing at Martin's jokes and nodding when he talked.

Martin's Dad had a shipping business in Newcastle with an office in Sydney. Now Martin had come to Sydney to learn the way things worked here. He said he was just starting to get to know people and things in Sydney, but he went back to Newcastle to visit because his family and his regular girlfriend still lived there. He said it was good to meet some other pretty girls in Sydney, perhaps he would find a new girlfriend here. Lizzie felt he was hinting it might be her. She was flattered, though she did not know if she liked him enough for this.

Lizzie found Martin interesting and easy to talk to, he seemed so confident. But there was something a little pushy about him and his friends seemed too much in awe of him. However he was well mannered and charming so she found herself enjoying his company.

Soon they went into the water swimming. The rest were all really good swimmers including Julie. Lizzie was glad her Dad had taught her to swim when he was alive; she had been a good swimmer when she was little. But she had not had much chance to practice since then. So, while she could swim well enough, she did not have the smooth and polished stroke to cut through the water that the others did.

However it did not stop her having fun, she joined in all the games. She went with the fun of it when the boys tossed her in the air and caught her, even if it seemed that they tried to touch her in private places when they caught her. But she was starting to realise that this was how grown up boys and girls played and, if Julie did not object, why should she.

In the mid-afternoon two of the boys went off and came back with a huge bag of fish and chips, along with big bottles of soft drink that they all shared. Then they turned to talking about their next outing together. The next Saturday night there was a party in Vaucluse that most of them were going to. It was at another friend's house. "His Dad is seriously rich and he throws the best parties," Carl said.

Before she knew what was happening Lizzie was being pressed into coming along. She said, "I don't think Mum will let me and I don't have the nice clothes that the rest of you do."

Carl said, "Surely Julie can lend you a dress, you are both about the same size, and you can say you're going to stay at her place and she can say she is stopping over with you, that way neither lot of parents needs to know. Then, the next day you can both go home to your own places and no-one will be any the wiser."

Lizzie felt a bit doubtful but now Julie joined in enthusiastically, "Yes let's, why not, no one needs to know and what harm can it do. It sounds like such fun."

So Lizzie found herself agreeing and feeling secretly excited at the prospect, as well as at the clever trickery it involved.

They arranged to meet at the City Town Hall steps next Saturday, at seven in the evening. It was agreed that Lizzie would first go over to Julie's in the mid-afternoon, for a planned sleep-over. They would both get ready there. They would say to Julie's parents that they were going to the pictures in the State Theatre in Market St and would catch the bus home to Lizzie's place where they would stay for the night.

Instead Martin and Carl would pick them up in a car at Town Hall and they would go out to Vaucluse from there. Carl had a cousin in a house in Paddington, with spare beds. So they would come back there, after the party, to sleep before they went home the next morning.

Soon it was Saturday, and Lizzie was packing to go to Julie's place. She felt a pang of guilt, she tried not to lie to her Mum, and this sneakiness did not feel right. There were often things she did not tell her, but she tried not to tell outright lies. And yet now she was doing just that. But she pushed it away, she was just going out for a good time, she was doing no harm. It was what everyone did at her age, easier than trying to explain to parents their need to go out and have fun with others

Chapter 4 - Not Supposed to Happen This Way

It was great fun getting ready; Julie lent her a really smart, low cut pale yellow frock, with a jacket to cover it up, while they were leaving her house. They locked themselves in Julie's room and did each other's hair, or at least Julie did Lizzie's and she tried to help a bit as Julie did her own. Then Julie got out her make-up and got to work making up their faces. She was obviously highly practised at all this. Lizzie did not have much idea or skill, sometimes she used her mother's lipstick but that was about the limit.

However Julie had it all, eye shadow, mascara, skin tints and so many colours of lipsticks. They experimented for half an hour and Lizzie found herself thoroughly enjoying this creative fun with her friend. They dawdled away an hour or two until at last it was almost six in the evening and time to go. There was a ten past six ferry from Birchgrove which would take them to Circular Quay and from there they would catch a bus up George Street.

So they called out their goodbyes and slipped out of the house. Lizzie was pleased that she did not have to walk past Julie's parents. They were sitting out the back. She did not lie as easily as Julie did, and she found it much harder to lie when actually looking at people.

It was just coming to seven on the Town Hall clock when they alighted from the bus. There was one of Martin's friends, Will it was, waiting for them. He led them around the corner into Clarence Street where the car was parked and the others were waiting. There were six of them, Carl and Julie got in the front with Martin and Lizzie went into the back with Will and Dan. The car's seats seemed huge and incredibly plush and she sank in between the two boys. The engine started and they were away, driving down the city then out along Oxford Street. Soon they were stopping at a big hotel. They all went inside to a quiet corner with lounge seats. The boys ordered beer and she and Julie each had a sherry. Lizzie had barely tried more than a sip of any drink before and she found the sherry strong but sweet and easy to swallow. On her second drink she could feel herself becoming light headed. After an hour they went on again. It was dark now. The lights and the world seemed to float by as they wound their way along a series of roads.

Then they were stopping at a really big house with lots of lights on. Martin took her arm and walked her inside where he introduced her to the host. Carl and Julie followed just behind. Dan and Will were a bit further back, staying together. Martin was good company, he knew lots of people and Lizzie found herself talking to other interesting people, she could feel her tongue loosening as the evening flowed along. There was lots of delicious food, like her Mum's party food, but so many more types, carried around by waiters on little silver trays. Now she found herself drinking glasses of champagne, a really good one that Martin had insisted she try. Every time she drank a bit someone filled her glass again. After a while she had no idea how much she had drunk.

But it was fun. Then there was music, a song by a new group called 'The Beatles' that everyone seemed to be playing and some songs by an American called Buddy Holly and lots more. Will had her up dancing, even though her feet got a bit tangled, then Martin had a turn, then someone else, then Dan, She could feel herself getting breathless and giddy with all the swinging around. Then Martin got her up for a slow dance and she could feel his strong hard body pushing up against her as they danced really close together. Then it was another wild rock and roll sort of dance. It seemed to go on forever.

Everyone was hot and breathless when it finished. She gulped down her champagne, finishing the glass. Instantly it was refilled and she drank this too because she was thirsty.

Martin led her outside, it was much cooler there. She leant into his arm as she walked along; she found it hard to walk straight by herself. For a minute they stood on the steps, looking out across the street to the harbour beyond, Martin with his arm around her shoulder and Dan and Will a couple steps behind. The world swayed in front of her.

Julie and Carl had drifted off to some other part of the party, she half thought she should go and find Julie and talk to her, but Martin had his arm firmly around her. It seemed too much effort to separate from him.

She felt quite fuddled from all the drinking, but it had been a fun night. She really felt like sitting down and resting, just for a minute. At the back of her mind she had a sense of deja vue, like she had been in this place before but she could not remember quite when. Then it came to her, Sophie, in the dream, had been standing down the path just in front of her. But she was not there now.

Next thing she knew Martin was saying to her, the car is just across the road, let's go and sit into it for a minute. Holding her firmly around the shoulders he led her down the path and across the road. She had another fleeting memory of the place in the path where Sophie tried to stop her, but she turned her head the other way as she went past to block it out.

When they got to the car Martin opened the back door and eased her in. Then he came in next to her, his arm now around her waist and his chin nuzzling into her neck. It was dark but the street light lit them. She realised he was trying to kiss her; she turned her face to look at him. He had a strange panting and desperate look on his face, like he was looking at her but seeing an object, part her, but not really her. He was also looking intently at the front of her low cut dress; she realised he was trying to look inside her top, and stare at her body. Even in her fuddled state it made her uncomfortable.

Next thing she knew Dan had got into the driver's seat and Will was in the front passenger's seat. She did not understand why they were there, but she was not thinking very clearly. Martin was trying to put his hand inside her top. She pulled it out. Then the car engine had started and it was being driven down the road.

She said to Martin, through her fuzzy brain, feeling uneasy. "Where are we going?"

He said, "I thought we would go for a drive to the beach around the corner. It is really quiet there at this time of night, and the view of the harbour is great from there."

As they drove her unease faded, what was the harm of going to the beach and looking out across the water. Martin was leaving her alone now. He was looking around the street as they drove, as if to see if there was anyone else out there.

Soon they came to a place with a big sign which read "Nielsen Park". It was an area of parkland and at one end the road curved around to the beach. There was no one else in sight and they had seen no one on the drive. Martin pulled her arm to bring her out of the car. He escorted her to the sandy beach where he sat down. He pulled her down beside him.

Then he pushed her onto her back and was pushing his body on top of her. She tried to wriggle free, but he was way too strong. Now he had put his hand under the bottom of her dress and was trying to pull her panties down. She realised now this was not where she wanted to be and that this was trouble.

She grabbed his hand and pulled it away. She tried to push him away, pushing as hard as she could. His arms were like a vice, and his body was really heavy in top of her, she could barely move.

She said to him, "If you don't stop now I will scream."

He just laughed and said. "Boys, she is threatening to scream; maybe we will have to gag her before we finish this."

Then he grabbed her mouth really hard, crushing her lips together in his hand. He said, "Time to stop fighting or we really will hurt you, much better if you just lie back, open your legs and let it happen. You didn't think we brought a pretty little poor girl to a party just to admire her did you. Now it is time to reward us back for being nice to you"

She shook her head, she could not just let this happen, she struggled even harder and started to call out for help.

Suddenly all three were holding her. One put tape around her mouth; the other held her from behind; the third picked up her kicking legs and pulled her panties down, part tearing them. He held them in the air. "Look what I have got boys; we might keep this as a souvenir, to remember tonight with Lizzie."

Martin took his pants off. Will and Dan held her down on her back, with her legs kicking frantically in the air, her dress pulled high above her waist and her body naked below. One pushed his finger into the place where her legs met. She tried to bite a restraining hand; the hand grabbed her hair and wrenched it violently. She felt she would pass out from the pain and shame of this. They wrenched her legs apart, leered at her nakedness, and touched her there some more.

"What do you know lads, still a virgin, must be our lucky day!"

Now Martin was on top, pushing into her. It really hurt. She felt something give, like a rip inside. Now he was moving and groaning, as if in huge pleasure. She felt sick. It hurt her inside; it was supposed to be nice, not like this.

After a while Martin stopped moving and pulled off, she could not bear to look at him, she had trusted him. Then Dan took his place and for five minutes he did something like Martin did, finishing with a cry of pleasure. Martin whacked him, "Keep quiet you goose". Now Will took a turn, by now she was trying to close off her mind and go somewhere else, where she could not feel it and did not let herself believe it.

When Will had finished they all sat there, next to her, congratulating themselves on what a good thing she was, how well they had done to find her and bring her here. She curled on her side, facing away from them, trying to cover herself. She hoped it was over.

But it was just a brief respite. Soon they all decided they wanted second turns. Lizzie was trying not to cry. With her mouth taped closed she could barely make a noise, but little whimpering sobs were coming out of her.

This was so awful, why had she let herself come, why did she think Julie was her friend, why had she not listened to Sophie? She wanted it to end and to get away from here.

Finally it was over; they took the tape off her mouth. They said that it would be stupid to scream now, that no one would believe her if she said what had happened. They would say she was drunk and had agreed and enjoyed it; now she was just trying to change her mind.

She knew it was hopeless and she did not want anyone to know. She dressed and when they were only half watching, in their smug self-satisfaction, she ran off into the dark night.

There was a half shout and someone chased her for a few paces. Then he tripped and fell, grunting and cursing, into the bushes. After that there was just silence as she slowly edged away from where they were. A few minutes later she heard the car start and saw headlights sweep the sky as they drove away.

She walked through the night for hours, only half knowing where she was. Before long she came to a road which she followed, and then another road, walking with no purpose and turning at random.

Dawn saw her at the edge of Centennial Park; from here she knew her way home. She found a tap and washed and cleaned herself as best she could, her dress and outer clothes seemed fine, just a few marks which she rubbed away. Her panties were torn and covered with blood, so she threw these in the bin.

It hurt down there when she walked, but if she went slowly it was not too bad. It seemed to take hours but eventually she found herself at the front of their house in Smith St, Balmain. She knew her Mum and David would be at church, she had heard the church bell ring from the bottom of the street. So she slipped around the back, let herself in, bathed herself and put on clean clothes. Then she lay on her bed and cried herself to sleep, overwhelmed with shame and a hurting body.

She heard her Mum and David come home but begged to be left alone, saying she had a headache. Two hours later came a knock on the front door, it was Julie. She asked if Lizzie was home. Her mother brought Julie to the bedroom and asked her to be quiet because Lizzie had a headache.

Julie closed the door and came and sat next to her on the bed. "Where did you go? Martin and the other boys said you felt sick and decided to catch the bus home. I did not know whether to believe them; there was something funny, a sort of smirk about the way they said it. I was too drunk and fuzzy to really question them. But here you are, safe and sound, so they must have been right. Are you OK now?"

Lizzie turned her face away and buried it in the pillow, what was the use of saying anything? Like they said, no one would believe her. She felt so ashamed, she wanted to pretend that it had never happened; she wanted everyone to go away and leave her alone.

Julie kept trying to talk to her and she kept turning her face away, struggling to hold back the tears. Finally Julie said. "There is something wrong, isn't there? Why won't you tell me? I am your friend. I thought you were my friend too; friends tell each other these things."

Lizzie replied. "I don't want friends like you, rich spoilt kids, who have never had to work for anything, who think they can do whatever they like and get away with it. I hate you and I hate all your friends. I just want you to go away and never come back. Go now, please, and don't come back here anymore."

Julie had a shocked and stricken look on her face. Lizzie realised what she had said had really hurt her; it was not really Julie's fault what had happened, she just did not understand what it was like to be poor and have to fight the world and all the rotten people who lived in it. Julie trusted people and did not realise how some people were all bad inside.

But now Lizzie was determined to be left alone. Friends like Julie would only cause trouble, and still more trouble. Julie looked like she wanted to plead or ask more. So Lizzie hissed. "Just go, like I said, I don't want to talk to you again, ever."

The door closed. Lizzie was alone.

The next day a note came from Julie, saying she was sorry for whatever she had done and still really wanted to be friends.

Lizzie burnt the note, but put her own note inside the envelope. 'Leave Me Alone!!' She marked it, 'Return to Sender'.

After that she did not hear from Julie any more.

She also stopped talking to her other friends from school. She did not want to go out; she did not want to see other people. She stayed in her room during the day trying to block out what happened by reading books or just staring at the walls. She refused all her other friend invitations, telling them she had a headache or felt sick.

A week later she started her job in the factory in Pyrmont.

Chapter 5 - Lizzie Runs Away

Lizzie found the work at Pyrmont was an escape from sitting in her room at home, talking to no one. She was glad when it started on the Monday, a week after it happened.

The work was boring but not hard and the people were friendly even though there was little time to talk, only a ten minute morning tea and a half hour lunch. Lizzie had the job of packing boxes of appliances; putting each appliance in its own box, making sure there was an electrical cord, then sticking the right label on the box. She sat alongside three other middle aged women who did the same thing. Another lady stacked all the boxes into a much larger box. When each large box was full it was put onto a conveyor belt which carried it to a storage room below. Here they stacked the large boxes for delivery to shops.

Lizzie was happy to have this job, the work occupied her mind and body without needing to think or talk. They all needed to watch what they were doing and go as fast as they could. They had a quota to meet and got a small bonus for extra production, which was important to the other ladies. So it took all Lizzie's concentration to keep up and do her share. As she got faster the ladies became friendly; they could see she was trying as hard as they were and earning her keep.

They started to tell her little things about themselves and their families and asked her about her own family. She said that she had a mother and small brother but her father was dead. Now she needed to earn money to pay her share. They all understood this, for all of them life was hard too. Each Friday one of the ladies brought little cakes in for morning tea. When her turn came around Lizzie did this too, using her Mums chocolate cup cake recipe. After this they treated her like one of them and Lizzie gained a sense of camaraderie if not friendship.

A few boys at the factory tried to talk to her. She knew at least one wanted to ask her out. But she repulsed them all, turning away from them with dismissive indifference.

At home Lizzie made a special effort to talk to her Mum about ordinary things and play with David. But she had stopped going out, even at weekends when not working. She stayed in her room and declined all invitations to do other things. She had become silent and solitary, sometimes walking out by herself, but avoiding all other contact. She would no longer go to church with her mother and brother. When they suggested this she had a manner which was cold and hard, leaving no room for argument. Her mother knew something was wrong but was unable to penetrate Lizzie's fiercely guarded privacy, so she left her alone.

A month went by and it was Christmas. She used two of her saved pounds to get a present each for her mother and David, and sat politely with them while they ate their Christmas dinner, but avoided going out or talking to neighbours. Another month passed, then another and then it was three months. The angry hardness remained unchanged, but now people had stopped trying to engage her and just left her alone. The only people she talked to were the other women at her work and her mother and brother and, even then, the conversation was limited to a few polite phrases.

After about three months Lizzie started to wonder why she was not getting her periods any more. She did not know much about babies, but had a vague awareness that what had happened to her could make a baby. She tried not to think about it, determined not to remember that night, let alone think about any consequences.

By four months she could not longer hide from herself what was happening to her body, her tummy was starting to push out and she could no longer pull it in, even though other people could not see this yet. Her breasts were also tingling and had changed shape and colour. But as no one else could see it, she tried not to think about it or what the future would hold. By five months it was becoming hard to hide, particularly from her mother and her friends. She knew now, for definite, that a baby was growing inside her, she had not been to the

41

doctor or talked to anyone about it, but when she looked in the mirror there was no hiding it.

She wore loose fitting clothes that made it hard for others to see the changes. She kept even more to herself, staying endlessly in her room at home. She now started to feel little movements inside her and realised these were baby movements, this was a living person not some horrible object.

At first she had felt hatred for this thing, which symbolised these men's brutality and her loss of innocence. Now she found her attitude was changing, she could no longer sustain this hatred as she felt this moving life grow. It was not the fault of this poor little hidden creature. Gradually it became her new friend, she started to tell it stories and sing it songs. In a strange way this gave her solace and made what happened easier to bear.

Now she knew this could not go on for much longer, once the people at the factory found out she would be asked to leave. She also knew that, if her Mum and other people she knew in Balmain found out she was expecting, she would be made to go to a place for unmarried mothers and give the baby up for adoption.

While she and her mother had never talked about pregnancy and babies she had heard the women at church talk about these things and her mother was a regular church goer who seemed to share their beliefs so it was clear to Lizzie what she could expect to happen.

She could not bear the thought of this. People had betrayed her trust. But it only made her more determined; she would not desert and betray this child, she would find a way to keep it for herself.

She had heard the stories of what happened to other girls who got in the 'family way', pregnant, they were made go and work at the local nunnery until their babies were born, then the babies were taken away and adopted out. She had heard these stories, going around the school and amongst the neighbours, and she half knew a couple other girls around her age this had happened to, they had dropped out of school and largely disappeared to have their babies. She had seen them later, without any child, somehow seeming profoundly sad, but still carrying their shame in the mutters and gossip which followed them. She had never thought much about how it must feel before. Now a sense of outrage began to grow in her, the idea of being further punished for this awful thing that had been done and that another innocent life would also be made to suffer, torn away from its mother made her sad, angry and determined.

So she began to form a plan, She knew that in another month or two the secret would come out and she must be ready to go away before then. She did not think she could stay in Sydney. It was a big city, but sooner or later she was bound to run into someone who knew her and would have to explain what she was doing. Then the baby would be found out. They would, almost certainly, take it away from her, saying she was too young and could not support her own child.

She knew she needed money to go away. Since she had been working her mother had insisted she keep half her wages. Now she had over forty pounds in the bank. If she kept working for another two months she would have almost seventy pounds, it did not seem like a vast sum, but it would have to do.

She turned her attention to where to go. If not Sydney could she go to a country town or another city?

She rejected Newcastle out of hand, Martin came from there and she could not bear the thought of seeing him again, or him seeing her, particularly now, with her bloated belly. She doubted it would occur to him that it was his; no doubt he and his friends had done the same to other girls before and since. She knew she was not their first conquest; they were far too smug and sure for that. But it would justify his opinion that she was a woman of low morals who would do it with anyone. Plus she had a burning hatred for him; she thought she might try to stick him with a knife if the chance came. Better not to go there.

Other country towns were not a real option; in them everyone knew everyone else's business and gossiped about it. So that left big cities like Brisbane, Adelaide and Melbourne. She preferred the idea of

Melbourne; it was easier to get to with the train and it was bigger than the others.

And, though it was a small thing, her mother's brother lived there. She had liked him the couple times she had met him as a little girl, she had his address from the Christmas Cards he sent. Even though she did not intend to see him or let him know, it was comforting to have a family member in the same city if things ever got really desperate. She was sure, deep down, that if she really needed his help, he would not turn her away.

So that was it; when the time came and she must leave she would already have her bag packed with things to live on, a few clothes and some packets of cheap biscuits for the trip, so that she could conserve her precious money.

She found an old battered bag in the cupboard, something she thought her mother would not miss, and put in it as many of her spare clothes as she could manage to do without. Alongside these she placed the new dress her mother had bought her, the one really nice dress she owned, even though it did not fit her now that her stomach had got big. But hopefully she could wear it again one day and send a photo of her and her baby to her Mum to let them know she was OK when the time came. She took her few other precious things, the old purse from when she was eight, a couple trinkets of jewellery, a faded photo of her with her Mum and Dad when she was little and a couple of her favourite books. That was enough; she had to be able to carry the bag easily.

Next morning when she got to work she placed this bag in her locker. That way, when they gave her notice and sent her away, she could leave without going home; better that way.

The work continued and somehow she managed to keep the baby hidden from her mother and David. Her other friends had given up on her so there were no problems there.

By about six months she had a sense that the ladies working with her probably knew but, whether out of kindness or something else, they said nothing. Now she avoided going to places where other people met, she would stay and have her morning tea and lunch in the work area and try to get a bit of extra work done to boost the bonus, every little bit helped.

By seven months she realised she was living on borrowed time; it was getting really hard to hide. Only by coming directly to the factory room where they worked and wearing a big overcoat, could it remain unknown. She was sure the other ladies knew but they chose not to ask her.

One day a factory meeting was called for everyone to attend. Lizzie did not want to go, but was told she must. She put on her coat. It was a warm in the factory, even though it was cold outside and she could feel herself uncomfortable in the heat. She stood as far to the back as she could, in a corner behind some boxes, to keep out of sight. Union officials were talking about safety at work and the danger of unprotected machines. It went on and on.

Lizzie started to feel dizzy, she had been in a rush this morning and her breakfast had been missed. Now that the baby was getting big she found she needed to eat more and more often. She could feel herself begin to sway. She grabbed some boxes for support.

In her panic she dislodged a large box. It fell to the floor with a loud noise. Everyone stopped talking and turned to look where she was. Now she was really dizzy and was swaying for all to see. The people gathered round and a big man took her arm to support her. Someone else insisted on taking off her coat, protests were useless. She was led to a chair. As she was sat into it her swollen belly was there for all to see.

There was whispering, the secret was out. Eventually the meeting continued. At the end of the meeting the floor manager asked her to come to his office. He indicated to a chair. Lizzie sat down. He said to her, "You know it is a condition of employment that pregnant women cannot work here. You clearly should have told me months ago. So you have to finish up now."

He handed her a pay packet saying. "Even though I don't have to, I have paid your wages for the rest of the week, and the women from your group have come to me and asked that their bonus for this week is all paid to you, so I hope that helps a little. It is lunch in half an hour so you can stay until the end of lunch to say goodbye to your friends, but you must leave then.

Lizzie felt tears pricking her eyes, partly in gratitude for the unexpected kindness from this man and her fellow workers, partly because of a sense of loss and loneliness, knowing that her future support was torn away and from here she had to do this all on her own. Still another part of her felt relief, knowing the need to live a lie was over.

So she goodbye and hugged her friends, who could now openly pat her belly and give her best wishes for herself and her child. The she took her bag and trudged down Harris Street to Central Railway, from where the train departed to Melbourne.

At the ticket office she found that a ticket to Melbourne was twelve pounds and that the next train left after seven o'clock in the evening, so she had more than six hours to wait. She sat on a bench in the huge hall of the station.

She felt so on her own, daunted by the challenge of going to a strange city where she knew almost no one, finding a place to live and a way to support herself until her baby was born and then raising a child by herself while supporting herself. Part of her just wanted to catch the bus back to Balmain and tell her Mum and let her look after her, it would be such a relief not to have to keep this a secret from her anymore.

But she knew that this would result in her baby being taken away and she could not bear for this to happen. This person was now her friend and nothing would come between them.

She wiped her eyes with her hanky and steeled herself to be brave. It came to her what she should do this afternoon. Since telling Julie to go away she had a bad feeling about it. Now she could not bear to have this between them, still ruining their friendship. She had been really scared before that Julie would try to stop her having or keeping her baby.

But now that was past, she was leaving and it was past time for any interference or pity. She wanted to see her friend again, tell her she did not hate her, smile and laugh with her one more time and say goodbye; their lives were on different paths now that were unlikely to cross again.

Julie was staying at the Presbyterian Ladies College at Croydon. There was a train to Croydon; it took less than an hour from Central, it was a station before Strathfield. Once she got there someone could tell her where the school was. If she arrived just before when classes finished for the day and asked politely she was sure that someone would call her friend and let Lizzie talk to her.

So she went to the suburban train platform and waited for the next train which stopped at Croydon Station. Once there she got directions to the school. It was a long walk, particularly carrying her bag. But she had plenty of time. So she went slowly, resting on seats a couple times.

It was three o'clock when she came to the school office. Someone said that classes would be finished in less than half an hour and sent a message to Julie's class for her to come to reception when it finished. Lizzie sat and waited, lost in a dream of might have beens, as she watched these bright and pretty girls coming and going.

There was a familiar voice and a scream of delight. She looked around; her back was turned as she sat facing the other way. She got to her feet, her movements cumbersome. She turned to her friend, whose face was covered in an infectious smile of delight.

As she took it all in Julie's face crumpled, "Oh Lizzie, Lizzie, what has happened? Is this why you would not talk to me?

Lizzie suddenly wished she had not come; why did she think her friend should know this? She felt so shamed. She wanted to run and hide. She wanted Julie to stop seeing her this way and only to remember her the way she had been before.

But Julie did not stop; she kept coming and wrapped her arms around her friend. She hugged Lizzie to her, cradling her head as if she was the most precious thing in the world. Lizzie hugged her back.

Julie's face was stricken; it was as if her mind had taken her half formed suspicions of something bad happening on that night, and turned them into a sudden and coherent understanding. She kept her arms wrapped around Lizzie and now she was crying.

"Oh Lizzie, I am so sorry, I should have known, it is my fault. You never would have come that night, you never would have even met them, if I did not make you."

They walked outside, together, and found a seat in the shady garden. Now Julie was determined to know the truth, she made Lizzie tell it to her every part she remembered. She could feel a rage building in her friend and it scared her. Now she really wished she had not come and the story had stayed untold, but yet it felt so good to have her friend back.

Julie said, "I don't know how I am going to do it, but I am going to pay those bastards back for what they have done to you, some way, some day; that I promise you."

Then she said. "You are probably pleased to know I am not seeing Carl anymore. I really liked him before, but not after that night. I think he knew what had happened, or at least some part of it, but would not tell me. After I saw you the next day I tried to find out what happened from him but he would not give straight answers to my questions, and he still stayed friends with them.

"So, after that, when he asked me out I said no, and when he tried to get me to do things with him I kept saying no. He still keeps pestering me sometimes, but it does no good. Now I am really glad it is over with him.

"But that is no help now; I just wish I could do something now to help you." She opened her purse. It had fifty pounds of pocket money her parents had given her last weekend for the month. She put this money in Lizzie's hand. Lizzie tried to it push back, saying she had her own money from working, but Julie would not take it back.

Then Julie made her tell her about her plans, the train to Melbourne, how she was determined not to let anyone come and take the baby away. Julie wrote her address and telephone number at school and home on a piece of paper and told Lizzie she must ring or write as soon as she had a place to stay. In the holidays she would come and visit and, in the meantime, she would send more money if needed.

Lizzie nodded though she knew she would not do this. She had to make her own way from here.

Finally the time was up; they had sat and talked for an hour and a half. Julie must get ready for dinner and Lizzie must leave to catch her train. Julie asked the school to ring for a taxi to drive Lizzie to Strathfield where she could wait. She said she would pay.

So now it was down to a few last minutes before a taxi came. Lizzie wanted to do something to set her friend's mind at rest, to move her beyond the guilt. She took Julie's hand and placed it on her belly. For a few seconds they stood that way. Then a huge wave of movement flowed under their hands. Julie smiled in delight and Lizzie smiled too.

Lizzie said, "I needed you to feel that to understand. You see, it is not all bad, in fact it is not bad at all. Even though what they did was awful and I hate them for it, I cannot hate what was created. I have a new life living inside me. I love this person who I will soon meet. I will not let anybody or anything take this away.

"So hate if you must and pay them back if you can. But mostly remember we remain friends and this life in here is good. It must be loved and cherished, that is what matters."

With a final hug she was in the taxi. For the first time in many months Lizzie felt good and happy with her life. She only wished she could say goodbye to her Mum and little David before she left.

Chapter 6 - Melbourne Bound

Lizzie thought she was rich when she left Sydney, she had her friend back and she had over one hundred pounds in her purse. She knew she would not write to Julie for a long time, not because she did not want to stay in touch, but because she did not want her friend trying to pay for her new life. They both had to get on with their own lives in their own ways.

Her buoyant mood remained throughout the long night as the train slowly rattled its way south, with occasional station and farm house lights flashing by. But, as the light grew from the late dawn, normally a time when one's spirits lifted, and they approached Melbourne, reality started to take hold again. Where was she to go, how to find a place to stay and how to support herself, and soon to support a new baby?

She was dog tired and hungry, she had eaten oatmeal biscuits to limit her hunger, but she really wanted a hot meal, some of her mother's cooking. However she knew she would rapidly exhaust her limited money if she started using it for bought meals. In Melbourne she must find a place where she could cook for herself to conserve her limited budget. In the meantime she had to be strong and resist that comfort desire.

Her back was also aching, the baby was starting to really press down, and a night spent mostly sitting up had been uncomfortable. A few times she had managed to stretch out. But then other passengers would come onto the train and she would have to sit up again. Her body craved a hot bath, a hot meal and a warm bed.

At the main Melbourne station she spent a couple shillings on a map, so as to get her bearings. Then she asked people there if they could recommend any good and cheap places to stay. Someone suggested that she catch a tram to St Kilda, with lots of boarding houses she could try her luck there.

On walking outside she found it was a cold and dreary Melbourne winter day. A cold wind was blowing light misty rain. She wrapped her coat around her and shivered as she got directions for the tram to take her to St Kilda. An hour later she was trudging, bag in hand, down its main street, next to the beach. The view was dismal; grey ocean with broken white tops, barely a person in sight.

She tried a few places, boarding houses and the like, but the prices were higher than she realised. Most were upwards of twenty pounds a month, and in many she had nowhere to cook. She knew she must take somewhere soon, even if it only gave her a place for a couple of days. She could feel exhaustion starting to set in, her feet felt like lead and her bag like it was full of house bricks.

Finally she found something within her means, even though it was awful after her comfortable room at home. She was directed here by a lady at another house who seemed to have a little more sympathy for her than others had. It was sixteen pounds a month. It was a dirty little room outside the back of a shabby house, with a tiny gas burner in an alcove. The windows were broken, patched with sheets of board, and wind still came through gaps. However she was getting desperate. It was at least shelter and she thought she could fix it up enough to make it bearable.

The man who showed it to her was unshaven and smelt, wearing dirty clothes. However he seemed willing to take her money, and had either not noticed or chosen not to comment on her pregnant state which was less obvious in the heavy coat.

However, as she pulled out her money to pay, she heard the front door open. Someone called out; his wife came in, returned from shopping. She was a thin, mean looking woman, probably in her late forties, with a scowl on her face. She turned to her husband, who shrunk back under her glance. "Who is she? What are you doing, Joe?"

"I was going to rent that room out the back to her, you know the one you said you wanted a tenant for."

The woman looked at Lizzie suspiciously; perhaps she distrusted her husband with young women, though it was something more than that. Then she said, "Open up your coat, girl. Let me have a proper look at you." As Lizzie did her swollen belly pushed against the thin dress, it could no longer be hidden.

Then the woman turned to her husband and, with contempt, said to him. "What in God's name were you thinking? Can't you see she is up the duff with no husband in sight. And the baby can't be far away from being born. What did you think you were doing, offering her a home for bastard children? You must be joking if you think she can stay here. What about having a screaming and bawling kid in our house, what if something happens when the baby comes, did you not think of any of these things?"

Joe muttered something and shrugged his shoulders. The woman turned to Lizzie with a vicious look on her face. "I know the likes of you, spreading it around with anyone who wants it. Get your sluttish face out of here; if I see you again I will call the police."

Lizzie felt devastated and shamed. She did not much like this shambling man, but at least it was something. But the meanness of this woman made her quail, she knew how some people thought of unmarried mothers, but never had it been flung in her face with this nastiness.

As fast as she could she picked up her bag. She squared her shoulders, trying to hold a shred of dignity, and walked out. The lady slammed the door, with a vicious curse, behind her.

Lizzie could feel her self-control and sense of purpose collapsing. She stumbled as she walked down the steps to the street. She had to clutch at the rail to stop herself falling. Her belly gave a violent wrench and spasm as she hauled herself back. She groaned aloud, *that really hurt*, her hands involuntarily clutched her belly. She hoped it had not hurt her baby.

Then, adding insult to injury, her bag fell from her hand. It bashed into the concrete and popped the flimsy lock; her clothes and personal things spilled onto the dirty wet pavement. Two loutish young men walking down the other side of the street turned to watch. They whistled and clapped as she clumsily shoved her possessions back inside. Now, as she walked she had to hold her bag in her arms to stop the lock, which was broken, from springing open again.

She could feel tears trickling down her face; she took a deep breath to get a bit of self-control. Fifty yards down the street she saw a bus shelter. It seemed to be a bit protected from the wind and rain. She would walk there and sit down for a minute while she rested and tried to think clearly.

It took a lot of effort to walk the fifty yards, holding her bag this way, but she made it and fell back against the seat. Her whole body was trembling with a mixture of shame, hurt and exhaustion. She thought she would give anything, at that moment, just to be back in her own house; to feel her Mum and her little brother's arms around her; to be tucked into bed, like when she was a little girl, and to have that human comfort.

She tried to push it back but could no longer control her emotions. Soon she was crying. She turned her face away from the street, and buried it into her coat, sobbing in great gulping sobs, as her misery flowed out. As her crying eased, and she sat up, she realised that a middle aged woman, with a kind, plump face, had come into the bus shelter. She had a handbag and looked like she was waiting for the bus to come.

As Lizzie straightened this lady turned to her and said, "Can I help you dear? Seems like you are in a spot of trouble?"

In a gulping voice, trying to compose herself and not cry, Lizzie explained her situation. She tried to talk calmly but it all came out in a rush; that she had just come to Melbourne, that she needed a place to stay, that she had some money, but not very much, and that she thought she had found a room but when the lady saw she was expecting a baby she sent her away.

Now she needed to find somewhere before it got dark, but she had tried so many places and it was getting late and she was just too tired to keep looking. By the end she thought she would start crying again. But with a big effort she pushed a hanky into her mouth and made herself sit up straight.

The lady looked at her with real kindness. "I wish I could help, God knows you need it. But I have full house at the moment. Still, if it comes to that, we will make up a bed for you on the verandah. That will see you right for a night or two."

Then she thought hard. "I think I know someone down the street another hundred yards who could help; Evie, at Number 120. I would come with you now, but I must catch this bus which will be here in a couple minutes. Anyway why don't you try there, I hear that she has a room that has just come vacant.

"Tell Evie, Evie Mackenzie that is, that Sylvia suggested you come there. If she cannot help you, come back to Number 76, that's our place, just over there, I will be home in about an hour" she said, pointing. "At least we can fix you up for the night, give you a hot meal and a bath."

So Lizzie walked on down to Number 120. It no longer seemed so hard, now that she now that she had some self-respect again. Number 120 was a large ramshackle house, a street back from the bay. The lady who opened the door was old and frail looking but seemed friendly. When Lizzie mentioned Sylvie's name she positively beamed.

She said, "Well hello dearie, it looks like you need to sit down for a bit. You look done in, trying to walk around with a bag, in your condition, in this awful weather. She brought Lizzie to the kitchen and gave her a cup of tea and slice of fruit cake before asking what it was she wanted.

Lizzie explained that she had just arrived in Melbourne and needed a place to stay for at least three months and could not afford anything too expensive. The lady said she only had one room available at the moment. It was in the basement and not very fancy. There was a share kitchen at the back and a share bathroom on each level. Her normal rate for short term was a pound a night or six pounds a week. For a long term stay she was prepared to come down to eighteen pounds a month, provided it was for a full three months and was paid in advance, with an extra month for a security deposit.

Lizzie did her sums in her head, assuming that the baby would come in two months and she needed a month after before she could get some work, then the seventy two pounds asked would leave very little to buy food with.

Yet she must have a place to stay, she could not sleep out in this weather, and the day was two thirds gone, plus she was so tired that she did not think she could walk any further. Also she liked this lady, she seemed genuinely kind.

She was about to agree, too tired to bargain. She started to pull out her purse, to double check then count out her money. She could see the lady looking at her and considering.

The lady said to her, "I can see you are a polite and well brought up young woman. I don't want to know how you came to be in this condition, but you clearly can't stay out walking the streets into the night. I presume you need a place to stay, at least until your baby is born, and you can find some regular work.

"I will tell you what, I could come down to fifteen pounds a month if you could do a few odd jobs for me each day, mainly to make sure the kitchen is left tidy, with all the dishes washed and the floor swept or mopped at the end of each day. Can you manage that?"

Lizzie nodded her head; those extra pounds would make a huge difference to her feeding herself until the baby was born.

The lady brought her down to the room and, on the way, showed her the kitchen and bathroom. None of it was fancy but it was clean. The bedroom had high side window and otherwise just stone walls. It was cold, but there was a made up bed with two blankets and a cover, plus a cupboard, a small desk and a chair.

Lizzie said that she would take it and thanked the lady for her kindness.

"Evelyn is my name she said, Evelyn Mackenzie, but you can call me Evie, that's what most people do."

Lizzie introduced herself. Then she said, "If it is alright I will have a lie down for a while, I am really tired."

Evie replied, "Well of course, what I suggest is an hour or two of sleep then a hot bath. Then, if you come upstairs, I have a pot of hearty soup cooking away. It is for dinner for those guests who need a meal. I don't normally provide dinner to my long term guests, but tonight a bowl of hot soup and a couple slices of bread is exactly what you need to nourish you and your baby. So tonight I would like you to be my guest and join me for a meal. After that I will let you look after yourself."

Lizzie felt like crying again with relief at this further kindness. The lady left and Lizzie started to unpack her few things, determined to create a sense of order in her new home before she allowed herself to sleep.

A minute later there was a knock on the door. Evie was holding out an object wrapped in an old towel. I know it is a bit cold down here so I have brought you a hot water bottle, it will warm up the bed and help you to get a good sleep. She also held a book, with ruled lines. This is my guest book. I just need your name, date of birth and a contact address for a relative should I need to contact anyone, just in case anything happens to you. "You can fix me up in the morning with the money."

Lizzie wrote down her details, then insisted on paying, taking out the sixty pounds and passing it over. Evie looked at her details, "I will give you a receipt tomorrow. What a brave young thing you are, off on your own to have a baby and only 15 years old."

Chapter 7 – On the Street

Lizzie slept most of the next morning. Evie came down at eight in the morning with a cup of tea and a big bowl of oatmeal porridge saying, "I thought this would help you get off to a good start, just bring the bowl back to the kitchen and give it a rinse when you are finished.

"I will be out for a few hours but if you are looking for the shops to buy food the best place is about half a mile down along the bay street then turn back inland where the tram turns down. It's only fifty yards down that road, you can't miss it. Tell them Evie sent you and they will give you a good price. If you have a bit to carry, you will find a trolley upstairs, just inside the front door. You can use it to wheel things along, I find it makes the trip much easier."

Lizzie had intended to go shopping as soon as she had finished breakfast, but feeling warm and contented from breakfast she decided to lie back into bed for a minute. She snuggled under the covers. Next thing she knew it was nearly lunchtime. Even then it took a real effort to get herself out of bed. She knew making a good impression with Evie was important; she would do her bit to create it.

So she got up and tidied the kitchen until it shone like a new pin, then found the trolley and headed for the shops. She bought big bags of flour, rice, some sugar, a tin of milk powder, a block of cheese, bags of potatoes, carrots, onions and a cabbage, all of which were at a good price.

Then, conscious of her need for fruit and meat for a healthy diet, she bought a bag of apples and another of oranges. She was not sure what meat to buy, it all seemed expensive and without a refrigerator it would not last too long.

She asked the butcher what he would recommend, saying that she needed to mind her money. He suggested some lamb neck chops, saying they would make a good stew, and this would keep for a few days in the cool weather. It was clear he gave her a lot more chops than she paid for and she said so.

He just grinned at her and said, "Well we need to feed both you and that baby; you are looking thin and you need to be eating for two.

By the time she was home Evie had returned. She told Lizzie, beaming with pleasure, what a good job she had done in cleaning the kitchen. Next thing Lizzie knew they were sharing another cup of tea and cake.

Almost without intending to she found herself telling Evie about her life, not exactly about how the baby happened but enough so that Evie understood there was no man to help her, and that she was determined not to give the baby up for adoption.

So a friendship was born and as the weeks passed Lizzie gained a sense of security and comfort. More and more she ate meals and did other things with Evie.

There was something so kind and calm about Evie, sure she was thin and old and her hands shook a bit, but she was kind and gentle, the kind of person she pictured her own grandmother might have been. And she was surprisingly non-judgemental about the younger generations, rock and roll and all that and the way the world in which she lived was changing.

Evie had never had children of her own, she had been engaged at the start of the First World War but the man had never come back, his fate unknown. She had tried to find out what happened but all they could ever tell her was that he was sent to the Somme and, along with thousands of others, was presumed dead, though really he just vanished, probably one of innumerable bodies in the mud.

Evie said that ever since he went she had always regretted not giving spending those last few nights with him before he went away. She had always wondered, if she had, whether a child may have come, some part of him to remember and cherish later. But one could not remake ones choices. So, after the war, Evie's life had drifted by without marriage or children ever coming. She inherited her parents' house when they died, and her only brother had died ten years ago.

So, with a large house and no family of her own, she had starting taking in boarders, mainly to pay for the upkeep of the house, but also to give her money for holidays and doing other little things she liked. She said that, while she was not wealthy, she had more than enough to meet all her needs.

Now she treated Lizzie like the daughter that she might have wished for. To Lizzie this lady seemed to have become the kind grandmother she had never known.

Evie's only relative was a nephew, her brother's son, Jack and, even though he lived nearby, she did not see him often or even like him. She told Lizzie that some came out as bad pennies and that, ever since he was little, he had a mean streak.

Evie arranged for a midwife to examine Lizzie, someone she could trust not to bring in the authorities. It appeared that her pregnancy was normal and the baby was well grown.

Lizzie's pains came three weeks before the due time and the midwife was called, all was progressing fine, though the baby was a bit small. It hurt, but was less long and less bad than Lizzie expected. A couple hours later she was holding a small baby to her breast, the midwife pronounced the child perfectly healthy, if just a wee mite, who needed to be fed up.

Lizzie called her Catherine Julia Renford, taking her best friend's and her mother's middle names. The midwife wrote the names on the official forms, mother Elizabeth Anne Renford, aged fifteen years and eight months; father unknown.

Evie was so proud of mother and child; she could not resist telling all her friends, who came in an endless stream to visit, what a great mother Lizzie was and what a beautiful baby Catherine was. Lizzie declared to all that Evie was her new grandmother.

Soon after the birth Lizzie found a pen and paper to write a letter to her own mother to tell her the news. It was not an easy letter, but at least she now had some good news to tell.

When she had left Julie she had asked her, as a special favour, to go and see her Mum and, while not telling her the whole story, at least to tell her that she had gone to Melbourne because she was having a baby, and did not want people to try and take it away, and also that she would write to her once she was able to tell her something.

When the letter was done she put it in an envelope and was about to post it. Then she had a thought, *Perhaps she would she send her Mum a photo of her and the baby, with her wearing the dress her mother had bought for her birthday?* She also wanted a photo of her and Evie, with Evie holding the baby, like a grandmother. It would help reassure her Mum that all was well.

She asked Evie about this, and where they could get these photos done. She could tell Evie was thrilled with the idea. Later Evie told Lizzie she had arranged it for two days' time, at a photography studio in the Esplanade which fronted the beach. The three of them walked there so proudly, she wearing the lovely dress from her mother under her coat. She pushed her baby in a pram that one of Evie's friends had offered. The man set them up in his studio, in front of a large camera and with lights and flashbulbs popping.

At first Lizzie was worried about the cost, but Evie was determined to pay. She said, "It's not every day that I am blessed with both a new daughter and a granddaughter that feels like my own. I can't wait for your own mother to see these photos and know you are well and safe. Plus, it's not like I have so many other things I need to spend my money on."

They returned to inspect the photos two days later and decide which ones would be printed. They carefully examined all the contact prints with a magnifying glass and selected the six best ones. Evie ordered three copies of each, saying that she wanted them all in eight by ten inch size to go in a photo frame. They would be ready to collect in two days.

Evie would have ordered copies of everything, but Lizzie insisted this was wasteful; they still had the negatives and could print more, later, if needed. Even these photographs seemed a huge expense to Lizzie, almost twenty pounds, but Evie would agree to no less.

Before they left she paid for them all with a fifty pound note and gave Lizzie the change, saying Lizzie should use this to buy some clothes tomorrow, as a present from Evie to little Catherine. Lizzie felt as if her cup was overflowing with the stream of kindness from this dear old lady.

Next morning, with a list of baby shops to visit, and leaving her baby in the crib under the watchful eye of Evie, she headed out. It was nine in the morning, and the baby, having just fed and settled to sleep, could be expected to sleep until lunchtime.

This was Lizzie's first outing on her own and she revelled in the freedom. Her body shape was almost returned after the week since the birth. She felt well and incredibly pleased about the way her life had turned out. She selected two outfits for a tiny baby and two outfits that the lady promised her would fit a baby of six months. Then, as she still had enough money left, she chose one outfit to suit a child of twelve months. It seemed hugely extravagant but Evie said she was to spend every penny and not bring any change home.

She still had almost ten shillings remaining so she brought a delicious caramel tart for them both to share over lunch; Evie had a sweet tooth and this was one of her favourites. Feeling well pleased, she headed for home.

The house was quiet when she arrived which was unusual. As normal the other guests were all out during the day, gone to their various workplaces. But she was surprised as Evie often had the radio playing and could usually be heard banging around the kitchen, humming or singing to herself as she prepared lunch.

But today there was no noise at all. She called out to Evie as she opened the door, but there was no reply and no other noise came back. Lizzie was gripped by a strong sense of uneasiness, this did not seem right. She went through to where her baby was; Catherine was still sleeping soundly, breathing regular and cheeks a bright pink. Her anxiety eased slightly.

Perhaps Evie had popped out for a second and would be back before she knew it. But that did not seem right, she would not leave the baby and go off, it was just not something that she could ever imagine Evie doing.

However, after calling again, she made herself sit for five minutes to wait and see if Evie came back in. The hands of the old grandfather clock opposite the kitchen table moved with excruciating slowness as Lizzie sat there waiting.

Once this time had passed she decided she must investigate. She walked around the house, calling, going to every level; the silence was absolute. Finally she went to the door of Evie's own room and knocked; no reply.

The door swung open against her hand, so she looked inside. She spied a skirt and leg protruding from the other side of the bed. She hurried over. It was Evie, lying and not moving, though her eyes were part open. She might be trying to look at her but she neither spoke nor moved. Then she saw a breath.

Lizzie felt panic in her chest, something was badly wrong. Evie was alive, but seemed unconscious. She knew she must call an ambulance. She went to the phone and found the number for the police, written next to it. She rang and explained, the person said they would send someone round and would also ring for an ambulance straight away.

Ten minutes later she heard the siren coming down the street and at once the place was swarming, two ambulance officers placed Evie on a stretcher and took her out, a policeman examined the place where she had been lying to see if there was any evidence of something suspicious. Inquisitive neighbours gathered around outside the front of the house.

Lizzie asked the policeman whether she could go to the hospital with Evie. He said he would take her once he had finished his investigation but she had to remain here for now. So she went and picked up Catherine, who was due to wake, and placed her on her breast.

As her baby sucked away she tried to think what else she needed to do. If Evie and her were at the hospital she needed to let other tenants know what had happened. So she wrote a note and pinned it just inside the front door, where all could see, telling them that Evie had been taken to hospital and they would all have to attend to their own dinners.

The policeman took a statement from her. She told him what she knew, that she had left Evie in the morning to go out shopping and had returned to find her like this. The policeman, having conferred with the ambulance officers, said he thought that the old lady had a stroke. He offered to drop Lizzie, with her baby, at the hospital on the way back to the station.

At the hospital Evie was propped in a bed, with lines and tubes running from her. She showed no response as Lizzie came into the room. Lizzie found a nurse and the nurse called a doctor. The doctor explained it appeared Evie had a massive stroke; she was alive but with no signs of consciousness. It was unclear whether she would live or die, but even if she survived it was unlikely that she would ever leave bed again. He asked Lizzie if she was the next of kin.

Lizzie said she was not, but told them Evie said she had only one relation, a nephew who lived somewhere nearby. This man's first name was Jack, but she did not know his address and had never met him. The hospital advised they would ask the police to locate and contact him, but beyond this there was nothing anyone could do except wait and hope for a miracle.

Lizzie sat there for the afternoon, with Cathy on her lap, holding Evie's hand and talking to her. There was no response, either from her eyes or her muscles, but Lizzie persisted, wanting to tell this woman of the love she felt for her.

As the afternoon drifted away Lizzie slowly realised that Evie was in another place, beyond hearing or knowing of this world.

Finally, in the late afternoon, Lizzie gathered her things and, carrying her baby in her arms, walked slowly and sadly back to the house. There was a sombre mood in the house amongst all the tenants. Lizzie told them what little she knew of Evie's condition.

Next day she wheeled her baby, in the pram, to the hospital. The situation was unchanged, Evie hovered in a twilight world, but Lizzie and the hospital staff sensed she was slipping away. After staying with her through the morning and into the mid afternoon, Lizzie walked home with a heavy heart.

As she approached the house she suddenly remembered the photographs. They were due for collection today. So she diverted to the shop. The man had them ready in a rectangular cardboard package. She did not open them but carried them home thinking, *Tomorrow, if she still lives, I will bring them and hold them up in front of her in the hope she can see something.*

She was woken early the next morning, not long after daylight, by a policeman knocking at the front door. It was the man she had met two days ago. He told her, in a sympathetic manner, that Evie had died in the night. She asked what they had done with her body. The man said it had been taken to the morgue, until they were able to get in touch with her nephew, to determine the funeral arrangements. They had not managed to locate him yet.

All that day Lizzie sat around the house feeling lost, she could not think of anything to do. She did not have information about funeral arrangements that she could communicate to Evie's friends and she did not feel free to do anything further with Evie's things.

She had tidied up Evie's bedroom and other parts of the house, but she felt it was not her place to do anything beyond this. It was not her right to look through Evie's papers or pack up her things, even though she knew that Evie would have been happy if she did.

She was down to less than twenty pounds of her own money, so there was little she could afford to do in terms of making arrangements herself and, with Evie gone, she knew that she must search for work.

Evie had said that she would pay her to do house-keeping work here, when the baby permitted it, but this was no longer likely to happen. She knew she must get out and take some action now, move herself, but she was gripped by a sense of melancholy, almost despair, at the loss of this dear friend, despite knowing her for less than two months.

Late in the afternoon, as the last light was fading, there was a knock on the door. A big burly man, with a hard looking face, stood at the door. She asked if she could help him. He announced he was Evie's nephew, Jack, and the will had passed this property to him.

So now he was here to find out who was staying and what money was due to him.

He asked Lizzie who she was. It was said in a cold and dismissive manner; perhaps he assumed she was a servant. She told him she lived in the basement, with her child, and was the person who had found Lizzie and called the ambulance.

He snorted with contempt, "Better to have let the old bag die and saved the expense," he said.

Lizzie could feel a flush of anger rising in her cheeks, *How dare he talk about his aunt like that*, she thought.

He continued, "I am going to her room to see if I can find the rent books and see who owes me money. When is your rent due?

She told him she paid for three months at the start and still had over five weeks to go before her next payment was due.

He replied sarcastically. "That sounds like a likely story. Unless you can show me a rent receipt, I will give you until this Saturday, you can be out then, or you can pay me six pounds a week from here on, I am given to understand that was her standard rate."

Lizzie felt her heart sink. Somehow, after she had paid Evie the money at the time she moved in, a receipt had never got done. It was promised for the next day, but then as their friendship grew it had been forgotten. Perhaps Evie had written it out and left it in her own room, but she could not go there now to look. Within a few days of her coming here there had been an unspoken agreement that, while Evie lived, Lizzie would help with the house duties and, in return, she would have a place to stay for as long as needed, at no further cost.

She imagined she would stay on here for at least a couple years, until her baby was of an age where she could safely return to her mother in Sydney. Who knew, she might even try and get her mother and David to come and live here; the house had plenty of room for them all; Evie had hinted at this.

Lizzie stopped listening to the man in front of her as this conversation played out inside her head. She realised now he was talking to her again.

He said, "Did you say you had a child, where is your husband?'

Lizzie did not reply.

He looked at her with a knowing look, "Oh, so you are one of those, are you; mother to a fatherless bastard, making your living by working on your back. Well you can pay me in kind for services rendered, twice a week on your back, along with doing the house work; that should do it. We can begin that arrangement now, I am well ready to sample what you offer."

Lizzie flushed bright red. She shook her head.

"What, cat got your tongue, too good for the likes of me, are we. We will see about that. Well, you can think on it overnight. I will take a down payment of the first instalment in the early morning, when I come back. No need for you to get up to meet me, you can be waiting, full ready for me to take my pleasure of you in your own bed then; just leave your door unlocked for when I come. Otherwise I will see you out of here with no further delay."

With that he strode up to Evie's room. She heard the door slam behind him. Later, after she heard him leave, she decided she would look for the rent receipt. Then at least then she could ask for her deposit back as well as have some time to find another place. But the door was now firmly locked.

Lizzie did not know what to do, all night she tossed and turned with worry. Could she find a job that would allow her to keep her baby? She could not bear the thought of lying with this awful man and letting him do to her what those other men had done before. But she had a child to feed and nowhere to go. Was there any other choice?

Finally, with the dawn light, her mind was made up; she would rather go and live on the street than subject herself to this man. Even if she was reduced to doing what he asked of her, going with men for money, in order to feed her child, it would not be with him. Not after the way he talked about his aunt. Lizzie knew she may not be good but she was better than that; she felt resolute and her mind was clear.

So she packed her bag, tied it shut, picked up her child and went and gathered her meagre food and other possessions from the kitchen. She put them all in the pram, along with her baby, and walked down onto the street. Even though the pram was not really hers she knew that Evie's friend, who had offered it, would not mind her taking this one thing.

Just as she started to walk away from the house a man, in a large car, pulled up and walked towards the door. She realised, with a sinking heart, that it was the nephew, Jack, early as promised.

At first he barely glanced at her and she hoped she might continue on her way, unimpeded. Then he looked again, closely, and she realised that he had recognised her.

"Where are you going?" he said. "I came early, as I told you, looking forward to an hour with you before you rose from your bed. If you come back there now with me, I will treat you right."

Lizzie shook her head; she could not bear to talk to him.

He came and stood right next to her, looking into her face. He cupped her chin with his hand and turned it towards him. "You are a pretty little thing, and with such a young baby, how old did you say you are? "I am not sure you are of an age where they would let you keep a baby. I suggest you come back with me. Otherwise I will need to call the adoption people to see what right you have to this child."

Lizzie felt panic rise in her; she did not know where she could go or what she could do. She could not even bring herself to think about whether someone would try to take her child. But her biggest terror was to return inside and give herself to this man.

While she was on the street she did not think he would try and take her by force. But once she was inside she knew she would have no choice left but to do as he wanted.

Summoning all her courage she pulled her face away from his hand and slipped out of his grasp. Then, gathering all the dignity she could find, she walked away down the street.

He laughed after her with an evil laugh. "Wait until I tell the nuns about you. They won't wait to come and take your baby and give it to more deserving parents. They will want to make sure it does not grow up like you. Then you will wish you had done as I asked in the first place. With your baby gone it will seem that it was a small price to pay to give me some simple pleasure. And I promise you will not have to sell yourself to other men, not while you are with me."

Lizzie tried to block his evil voice from her mind. At last she reached the corner and turned away, out of sight. She felt sick with dread at what might be, but going back was worse.

Chapter 8 - A Baby and a Pimp

Lizzie pushed the pram, holding her child and all her worldly possessions, down to The Esplanade. It was another cold winter's morning but at least today it was not raining. The sun was trying to shine weakly and the wind was light.

She and Catherine were both wrapped up warmly against the cold. She had twenty one pounds in her purse and, now that she knew her way around, maybe she could find a job in one of the beachside cafes that sold drinks and hot food. Hopefully that would give her enough money to rent a room at night and buy food.

She did not know how she would manage with a baby, but perhaps, while Catherine was little and mostly slept, she could leave her in the pram out the back, safe, but out of the way, then attend to and feed occasionally between doing her other work. She would offer to do extra hours in return for any time off and inconvenience.

She tried one place, no vacancies there and no interest in having a woman with a small baby, a second place was similar. A third place actually had a sign looking for casual workers, but when they saw her baby the man behind the counter shook his head.

She could see another shop at the far end of the beach, a bit away from town, alongside a building next to the beach that looked like a club. She trudged there, not feeling hopeful. The lady who ran it seemed more sympathetic. She said she needed an extra pair of hands each afternoon, particularly from three o'clock to seven o'clock each evening, the time from after the schools came out until the dinner shift was finished.

The lady looked dubiously at the baby, so Lizzie said, "Could I just have a try for one night, then you can decide? If I can come back at three I will do the first day for nothing if you will only give me a go."

So it was agreed, the regular pay was to be a pound a day and, if she sold more than an agreed amount, she would get ten percent of her extra takings to keep as a bonus.

So she went and found a bed in a boarding house for the night, using up one more of her precious pounds in the process. She woke Catherine just before she left for work, and made sure she had a good feed, and then settled her to sleep in the pram. Then she walked back to the cafe, in time for her shift.

It was a busy; a clear cold afternoon and night, with people out along the foreshore. There was a brisk sale of hot fish and chips, meat pies and hamburgers. The time flew by.

It was past seven before the Catherine stirred; Lizzie gave her a quick feed then helped finish cleaning before she packed to leave.

The lady, Ruth, said "Well your baby is very good and there is no doubt you work hard so I am prepared to give it a go it for a month. She handed Lizzie two ten shilling notes, "That is your pay for the night, you have earned it. Help yourself to some left over hot food."

Lizzie took a hot pie and some chips.

For the next month, she worked there most nights. On average she made twenty five to thirty shillings a night. She also got some work stacking shelves in a shop, most days they would offer her two or three hours in the morning. Between the two jobs she was making just enough money for a room and food. A month on, towards the end of winter, she came down with a bad flu and could not work for a week.

Now her savings were reduced to ten pounds. She was starting to feel her situation was precarious, not so much for herself but for her ability to support her child.

Catherine was also becoming harder to manage; as she grew she stayed awake longer, her cry was getting louder and she was starting to grizzle if she was awake and unattended. She tried to keep her child awake in the night, once home, to help her sleep in the day, but it was hard. Lizzie was often tired and fell asleep herself after dinner.

She had started to make friends around the area, mostly young girls of a similar age to herself. She had particularly become friends with two girls who worked in a massage parlour that she walked past every day. Often they would sit out in the early afternoon as she walked to the beach café. One had a child a few months older than hers. First they said their greetings, then they started to talk about their children and soon they started to talk about their lives.

This girl, Rebecca, was surprising open and upbeat about her life. She was eighteen and had been doing this work for over two years. She had got pregnant after a year but the parlour had been good and helped her. First they had offered that, if she wanted an abortion, they would arrange it. Instead she said she wanted to have the baby and keep it. So, once she could no longer work, they gave her a room out the back, for no rent, provided she helped with domestic work and came back to her regular work as soon as she was able.

Rebecca told Lizzie about her work. Sure, she had to do the sex thing with a lot of men, but it was not so bad really, she treated it like an acting performance, as if someone else was doing it, not really her. Some of the men were quite nice and kind and gave her good tips. There was also good security, with two men who were always around, to make sure that no-one hurt the girls; in return she had to give one a bit on the side but he was nice and fun to do it with.

It was also good money and fitted around minding the baby. Most nights, when she worked her baby slept. In the daytime, they could do things and nap together. She said that, in the last six months since she had come back to work, she had managed to save well over a thousand pounds.

She was obviously angling to get Lizzie to give it a try. At first Lizzie politely declined but, as her money situation grew precarious, she started to think about it seriously. Rebecca even offered to share her room with Lizzie; "Then we could share the child minding, and the room is large enough for two," she said. This room was out the back of the parlour, separate from where they saw the gentlemen, which was good because if her baby cried it did not disturb others.

Finally, one day about a week after she got over being sick, when she had a really difficult day with Catherine, she saw Rebecca sitting outside one evening, playing with her baby. Except when she was sick,

Lizzie had not had taken a day off since she began work. She sat down in the empty chair beside Rebecca, just to say hello and catch her breath, before the rest of the walk home; that is what she was intending to do.

She was finding herself getting very tired by the end of the day since she was sick. She told Rebecca this. Rebecca said it was because she was getting run down with working so hard, not getting enough rest and not having enough money to buy good food.

Rebecca told her she was having a night off tonight; each week she had at least one night for herself and her baby, when she booked no clients. All her regulars were booked for other nights and there were enough other girls to cover any newbies. So tonight was her night off and she was enjoying the early spring evening, in the sea air, outside with her baby.

It seemed so much better than the life Lizzie was leading, she had no real money, no days off and, most importantly it was such a struggle, day after day, to care properly for her baby, buy the extra clothes Catherine needed, a better pram, all the other little things. She had a big list of all the things they both needed, but could not see how to get them; her wages only allowed living hand to mouth, they would not stretch to getting anything else.

Rebecca must have sensed the turmoil going on inside Lizzie. She put her arm around Lizzie's shoulder and hugged her. "You poor thing, you are just a wee mite and working so hard," she said. "Why don't you give it a try; it is really not so bad.

"When I was little, I was only fifteen; then two boys forced me to do it with them. I hated it. But right then I thought; why not do it on my own terms, and get paid for it. It is much better to get paid and protected rather than have horrible men or boys trying to take it by force, and give you nothing, except perhaps, one of these," Rebecca said pointing to their babies. "And these just use our money, not help pay the bills."

Lizzie laughed with Rebecca at this flash of humour. It felt good.

Rebecca went on, "Our pimp is actually a nice man. His name is Robert though we all call him Robbie. You will have to do it with him first, so he can make sure you are OK for the customers, but you will find him kind and gentle; you may even get to enjoy it with him."

The Rebecca took her hand and said, "He is in his room now, listening to music; relaxing before the night's work starts, why don't you come with me and I will introduce you. Then, if you like him enough to want to try, I will mind your baby while you go with him.

"After that, if you want to keep going, tomorrow you can bring your things round here and move in with me."

Lizzie felt panicked, she wanted to pull back and run away. All she could think of was how those men had held her down and laughed at her nakedness, before they hurt her. She did not want to be hurt again. Thinking of someone, a man, looking at her body without clothes, made her cringe inside.

But Rebecca just held her hand. She did not push her any further, she let her relax again. She said, "I know you are scared. I was really terrified first time. But then, when it happened, I relaxed and thought, it is really not that bad after all, is that all there is to it. Now I find it is mostly good. I could not enjoy my life without that part, and the money it brings.

Lizzie took a deep breath; what was there to lose, her life could not continue like it was and, if she had to do this thing with her body to survive, it was better that it be on her own terms.

So she nodded, "Yes, you can bring me up to meet him, and if he likes me enough, and if I don't think he is too awful, maybe I will try."

Rebecca handed her baby to Lizzie and said, "Just hold Andy for a second, I will run up and check to see if now is suitable."

As Rebecca disappeared Lizzie had another bout of panic. If not for her friend's baby, that she was holding, she would have got up and run off. But she could not leave this child alone, so she stayed, sat still and trembled inside.

Suddenly Rebecca was back, "Yes he wants to meet you; he needs five minutes before he is ready. Come to my room. We will freshen you up and tie up your hair."

That was it, the die was cast. Lizzie could feel her knees knocking as they walked to the back of the house and went into Rebecca's room. It was a big room with a large wardrobe full of lots of beautiful dresses and with a basin, tap and large mirror in a corner.

Rebecca got a washer and lathered it with soap. She handed it to Lizzie, "Clothes off and sponge off your body with this," she said.

Lizzie felt her courage start to fail again, but Rebecca stepped up and, in a matter of fact way, undid her clothes so they fell to the floor. She critically appraised Lizzie's body. "Not too bad, tummy still a bit saggy, but otherwise a good figure," she said. "The men will love your soft milky skin and slender girl body." Then she passed the washer and Lizzie dutifully cleaned herself all over, standing there in her panties.

"Everything off," said Rebecca, "clean all the places, particularly there," and she pointed. Lizzie blushed but complied. Rebecca handed her another clean rinsed washer. "Use this to finish off," she said.

Then Rebecca went to the cupboard and pulled out a soft flowing purple dress. From her drawer, she took out some lacy underwear. She handed these clothes to Lizzie who put them on under Rebecca's keen gaze. Now Rebecca brushed Lizzie's hair until it glowed and tied a matching ribbon loosely around it. With a final flourish she found a pair of matching shoes.

She stood Lizzie in front of the mirror to let her admire herself. "Anyone who does not think you look gorgeous does not know what a beautiful women looks like."

Lizzie could not help but agree; the transformation seemed miraculous; she could barely believe she was staring back at the same person. As Lizzie looked at this transformed woman, herself, but so different, she felt her confidence grow. It was not quite excitement, but an edge of anticipation for what was to happen.

"Now for a few finishing touches," said Rebecca. She applied lipstick, eyeliner and skin blush, followed by a light spray of perfume.

She surveyed her finished work and smiled with smug satisfaction. "Robbie is bound to find you exciting; he said he would only do it as a favour to me. I think he is expecting some plain Jane, but when he sees the gift I have brought him he will hardly be able to restrain himself, he loves beautiful women.

"My only advice to you is to try and make it all slow down, turn it into an act and imagine you are enjoying the act. Then it will be better for you both, perhaps real enjoyment will come."

Rebecca placed Catherine on the floor and Andy in his cot. "Be good, I will be back in a jiffy," she said to them. She took Lizzie's hand and led her up the stairs. She knocked on a door at the back of the second level.

A surprisingly young man opened the door; he looked to be in his mid-twenties. He had broad powerful shoulders but was otherwise slim. He had a nice face, close to handsome but a little weather beaten. Most of all he had a warm smile, which Lizzie really liked.

Lizzie smiled back, it was involuntary. Then she blushed. *What was she doing here?*

Rebecca said, "Look what a lovely present Santa has brought you. Robert, this is Lizzie, I will leave you to get acquainted." With that she skipped away down the stairs.

He gave a polite bow, "Actually I prefer if my good friends call me Robbie", he said. He invited Lizzie inside. He indicated a sofa where there was space for two. She sat down, perched on the edge.

He looked at her, keenly but kindly. "First, we need you to relax. Rebecca has told me you have a baby but this is your first time with someone else. So we need to take it slow. We will have a drink and you can tell me a little about yourself. Then, when you feel less awkward, we will see what happens from there.

He poured a small glass of mineral water and handed it to her. She sipped slowly.

"Tell me about yourself, how you came to Melbourne?" Lizzie briefly outlined a story about wanting to keep the baby, which her mother and the church ladies wanted adopted and, as a result, leaving Sydney. Now she needed to find a way to support herself.

He nodded understandingly. "Are you breastfeeding your baby?"

She nodded.

"That is important and you must keep it going for now, because one of the most important things is to make sure you don't have another baby, anytime soon. If you come and work with us we will also arrange other protection."

Then he untied the ribbon from her hair and said, "Give it a shake, I love a woman with hair around her face. Now he came over and took her hands. He lifted her to standing, right next to him. He cupped her face and gave her a slow and lingering kiss on the lips.

At first she felt shy and awkward, but then remembered Rebecca's advice about role playing. She responded, exploring his mouth back and enjoying the experience. It did something to her; it awakened a womanly part in her, giving her a warm feeling.

He walked her to the bed and indicated for her to stand just next to it. He reached down and lifted her dress over her head. Now she wore only lacy underwear. Again she felt self-conscious, starting to bring her hands to her front, as cover.

He took her hands and lifted them above her head, indicating he wanted her to stand that way for a minute. He unclipped her bra and looked at each breast, handling them gently and feeling their firmness.

It seemed strangely like a doctor's examination. She supposed in a way it was, a check for soundness and defects. Then he pulled her panties to the floor and indicated for her to lie on the bed, on her back, with her legs apart. He looked at this part of her carefully; more gentle touching and probing.

Then, apparently satisfied, he said "All appears healthy, I am sorry to act like a doctor but I needed to check. We have to be careful to protect our customers."

It was so clinical that she felt relieved; however she knew there was more to come.

He sat on the bed, and stroked her hair as she lay beside him. He said, "You are a lovely, sweet, innocent girl. While you obviously went with a man to get pregnant, I can see the rest of this is not something you have done before and it seems scary and foreign to you. However you are truly beautiful, with a lovely body and very sexy. Now you need to learn to use these things. I will try and help you.

"I need to see you try to use this appeal on me, to get me excited. Imagine I am the first and most handsome man you have ever seen and that you desperately want me to feel the same about you. With that in your mind, I want you to take off my clothes and to do it in a way that makes me mad with desire for you."

He stood in front of her and she sat up. His groin was almost in her face and she could see a bulge. She undid his belt and his buttons, his pants slid to the floor. Now she eased down the next layer.

She found herself curious to see what this part of a man looked like, the last time it had been dark and she had been trying to look away. She had never looked at a naked man this way before, and his maleness was in front of her face.

Without thinking she kissed this part and took it in her mouth. It seemed the right and natural thing to do.

He groaned and put his hands in her hair. Then he pulled her head back up. "I think you are getting it pretty well" he said. He pulled off his shirt. She looked at his rippling muscles and maleness.

She felt an ache in that woman's place of hers. It was as if her body knew how it was all meant to work. Her nervousness was gone now; she wanted this to keep going. Now he was kissing her and sucking her breasts. She arched her hips towards him, wanting more.

She saw him put a condom on. Then he was lying alongside her. She thought he would climb onto her and do the sex bit. But instead he caressed her body, rubbing her breasts and touching between her thighs. It was so pleasurable, and in return she stroked and touched his body and back, and then his maleness.

He rolled her on to her stomach and lifted up her hips. Now he was kissing that place. She started to pant and moan; there was no acting now.

He turned her back so she was facing him. "That's how it should feel. But if it doesn't that is how you need to act. There is nothing like a woman on fire to drive a man crazy."

Now he laid her on her back and placed a pillow under her buttocks. "That is to put you in the best position to enjoy what is to come," he said. He moved his body above her; she arched her body towards him as she felt him push into her. It felt huge.

Once he was fully inside he told her to lie there and get used to the feeling of him, and then to start to move herself against it, pushing up hard, and squeezing herself as tightly as she could. This would increase both their pleasure.

She moved her hips, tentatively at first, but it did really feel so good. Now she pushed herself hard and squeezed against him. He began to move too, coming up and down in time with her. She could feel tingles of pleasure spreading though her body. She felt her whole body was riding a rising wave of pleasure; he was the like the sea, pushing against her and pulling her along with him, as they both rose to the crest.

Just when she thought she could bear no more, she felt his fingers touching her, focusing on a small point. The pleasure was exquisite, she could hold back no longer, her whole body was convulsing.

Now he drove into her with incredible ferocity. There was a moment, suspended in time, when his body arched and shook, just like hers was doing. They cried out in pleasure together as they wrapped arms around each other's rigid bodies. Slowly it subsided.

They lay together, she stroking his head, like she would a baby. It was so much better than she had thought or imagined; a great unexpected pleasure.

After a few minutes he sat up and got dressed. He asked her if she had enjoyed it. She smiled back, a dreamy smile, and nodded. "More than I could ever have imagined."

"Me too," he said. "I have lots of girls, but with you it was something very special. When I saw how shy and nervous you were, at the start, I wanted to be the one to give the first real pleasure to your woman's body, to show you how to enjoy it," he said.

"Soon you will be doing this for a living, like I do. It won't always be good like this. But I want you to know and remember this; this is the way it should be, a thing to be enjoyed between a man and a woman, done with affection and tenderness and without shame.

"For this work you have passed with flying colours. A job is yours, from tomorrow, if you want. Sometimes we will do this again, together, just you and I alone; perhaps sometimes for a whole night, so we both remember what it feels like when it is really good.

"Now you need to get dressed and take your child home. I must get to work. My job is to protect all the girls here. They are entrusted to my care. I let all the clients know that, while I will not interfere with their ordinary pleasures, I can be there in an instant if needed."

As she walked back down the stairs to Rebecca, Lizzie considered her sudden initiation to this world. She had taken the first step to becoming a prostitute. Tomorrow she would take the next steps, repeating it with many other men.

Tonight was better, far better, than she imagined possible. She felt strange in her new found woman's body. Towards this man she felt deep love for teaching her to enjoy this joining and for bringing this part of her being alive that she had not known was there.

In this, her new chosen life, it must be something to enjoy, not fear. She knew it would not always be this easy or this nice. But doing this act was something she could manage; she could polish her performance and become a true professional as time went by.

Only one thing bothered her; it was the transactional nature. She would like to keep doing it with this one person she really liked, not to sell her body and this pleasure to whoever paid.

But there was no turning back now; she had run out of other choices. In her heart she knew that this was what the new Lizzie had become and she could never unmake it.

She made herself look at this new truth with honesty. She, Lizzie, was choosing to become a prostitute, she said this word over in her mind, *I am a prostitute, that is who I am, I will not pretend it is something else, it is a choice I have made, it is what I now do!*

Chapter 9 - A Kept Woman

Lizzie settled in to her new life easily. It was like, even though her body was used in a way she would not otherwise choose, her mind remained hers, alone and untouched. No longer was there unceasing anxiety of how to pay for the tiniest things, a bed or a meal.

There was a communal kitchen used by the girls and the two men who worked on the premises. Madam, a well-kept lady of about fifty, was also a frequent visitor. She appeared almost motherly in the way she approached the running of her establishment, or perhaps like a boarding school mistress. She knew all the girls by name; she would stand for no nonsense. There were no drugs on her premises and while they all shared a drink or two, before or after work, to help get in the mood, there was no all-night bingeing or slovenly behaviour.

She said, "Other places may tolerate this, but I will not." For those who did not like her way she said there were plenty other establishments they could go to.

She told them to act with pride, it was the world's oldest profession and one to be proud of; it met the needs of men. Her clients were valued customers who must be provided with a good, honest service.

There were strict rules around the money. While the girls were free to take tips and these were theirs to keep, the fee for service was paid to the Madam or her duty manager in advance. She took her share, the house took a share, the pimps, who she called 'house men', were paid theirs and each week the balance was passed over for the girls to each use how they liked. The house fee covered the food, the drinks and the rooms where they gave the service.

She insisted that there be no favourites, all the girls could have their regular customers, but they must also take an equal share of the new ones and, while they could go with the house men when they chose, this was not to be exclusive or take away from their availability to their clients.

Most of the girls were young, not much older than Rebecca, a few were older. Some had their own rooms here, others lived away, but they all would often gather for a meal and a chat.

They were all required to take off at least one night each week, and they could choose which other nights they worked, as agreed with Madam, and written in a book.

All were required to use contraception, previously it had been limited to condoms and diaphragms, but now this new pill was available, they were encouraged, but not forced, to use this. Madam called it personal responsibility. Lizzie chose to take the pill, but insisted her customers also wore a condom.

They all had a health check each week, done by another experienced person here, and they needed to tell Madam at once if they thought they had caught anything. She also made them all pay a regular visit to the doctor, whose visits she arranged each month. It seemed remarkably orderly and far from Lizzie's image of a seedy brothel. She knew she was lucky; there were many places that were not so good.

Rebecca, who she now called Becky, and she were like sisters, she was another Julie, someone who could be a friend for life. Rebecca had told her some stories of her early life, her father had also died young, but her mother had taken up with another man who she did not like and who had tried to molest her when her mother was not looking.

They both really liked Robbie and spent regular time with him, but it was not a jealous relationship, even though secretly Lizzie could feel herself a smitten by him, but they all knew the rules; kindness, affection but not exclusive love in this house. Those wanting that must move on.

One Monday night, a quiet night which both Lizzie and Robbie had off, she had spent a full night with him. It was really lovely, mostly they just talked, slept and cuddled together, with little Catherine lying in the corner in her pram.

She gathered her courage and told him about the night when she was raped, a thing no-one else except Julie had been told by her, not even Becky. She could feel anger in him about it. When she finished the telling he held her close, stroked her hair and said bad things happen in life and afterwards people have to move on with their lives like she was doing. She felt better and less bitter for his knowing; his strength was hers.

He told about his life before here, he had been a soldier in Korea, and watched two mates get blown apart. At first he had a death wish, wanting to kill all of them. But, as the months went by, he came to understand that he must not feed this hatred. It was a cancer; killing begetting more killing. Then he knew then he did not want to kill people anymore. So, as soon as a chance came, he demobbed.

He had come back to his home in Melbourne, but after life in the army he found it hard to settle into civilian life and do a regular job in some city firm, he needed life on the edge. He had stumbled into this work. He had always liked and enjoyed women, both their company and their pleasures. He loved all the girls and tried to give to them equally but, he had to admit, he had some special favourites, like her and Becky, even if he tried not to let it show.

In the small hours, when the only sound they could hear was each other's breathing, they made love with great tenderness; it was as if they were lost together in a place beyond all known worlds.

As they lay together, after, she asked Robbie if he had ever been in love with only one special woman, so that all he wanted to do was to be with that person.

Robbie told her that, before he went to fight, there had been a girl like that; he would not say her name. For all those months away fighting he had stayed true and imagined she was too. He had stayed in the barracks and remembered her and desired only her when his friends asked him to come with them when they went with other women. But when he came back from his first tour of duty he found she was with another man. Then he realised he was not special to her the way he had thought. So from then on he had taken his pleasures where they came, and enjoyed many women. But, each time, a part of him was kept, held back, lest he give himself too fully to another and not have it returned.

Then he said something which made Lizzie feel very special, "When I am with you, there is nobody else. That part of me, the part that stayed back before, it is not there anymore. All of me is lost in these moments with you."

Lizzie said in return, "I have not been with anyone else that I cared for so I cannot judge, but when I am here with you everything else stops being real, there is only here and now, and I never want it to end. I cannot imagine feeling way that with someone else."

At the end of their night Lizzie told him that if she ever had another baby she would like the father to be a person just like him, she was so glad he had been her first man after that awful night.

He replied, "If I become a father, I want someone just like you to be the mother."

Secretly she just wanted to go away with him, for them to have a life where it was just the two of them, and from these words she knew a part of him would have liked that too. But it was not to be, at least not in this time and place.

One day she visited Sylvia, Evie's old friend, to ask where Evie was buried. Sylvia walked with her to show her the grave. Sylvia said it was a disgrace; this man who had got all Evie's money had not even paid for a decent funeral or a proper headstone. A tiny plaque lay on the ground, with a few dead flowers that Sylvia and other friends had brought.

Lizzie found the undertaker and gave him one hundred pounds of her money to make a proper headstone from white marble. She would have done more but that was the limit of her spare money just then; perhaps she could do more when she had more.

A month went by; Lizzie felt that, once again, that she had found a new home. It was like she had felt with dear Evie. She had taken the name Luscious Lizzie, as her working name and now she had a regular following of repeat customers who booked her at least once a week.

She did not think much about what she did, her work; it was just an act that her body went through. When it was done, at the end of each night she showered and washed herself, this was now also part of her act, symbolically washing these memories away.

Catherine was now smiling at her when she woke up. Each night, once she was finished, she would wake her baby to enjoy a bright smile and give her lots of kisses. Sometimes, when she smiled at her, Catherine chortled with delight.

She now had three hundred pounds saved away and felt rich; others spent their money on clothes and finery, she spent only what she needed and saved the rest; the memory of her poverty was still too close to be wasteful and rely on good fortune.

Chapter 10 - Life Spins Out of Control

It was now mid spring, the days were longer and the sun was warmer. Most days, for an hour in the afternoon, Lizzie and Becky would sit on chairs in the sun at the edge of the footpath, while their children looked around and played. They both loved these times.

One day, as Lizzie was staring at Catherine, making little baby noises and trying to make her smile, she became aware someone had stopped in front of her, blocking the sunlight. She looked up. It was Evie's Jack; he was smiling at her, as if a friend, but the smile was not real. He started to say something. She nodded, picked up her baby and went inside.

Becky followed, a minute later. "What was that all about?" she asked. "When you left he tried to ask me questions about you, but I did not answer and left too. But he knows we both work here, he said so. As I was walking way he told me we could expect a visit from him; he looked forward to becoming a customer, meeting us both and really getting to know us in private."

Lizzie cringed inside. She had never turned a customer away, but she could not bear the thought of being with this man. She told Becky what happened when Evie had died and how frightened she had been.

Becky took a deep breath. She said, "We almost never turn anyone away, but I think, if we tell Robbie and Madam about him, they will understand and not let him visit you, perhaps not even me."

So they went and told the story, Robbie nodded, he seen this man around the town before, and knew he was trouble. He agreed he was a bully who could be violent, and may try to hurt or humiliate Lizzie. He said he would go and talk to Madam and seek her agreement that the business would refuse to let him visit either of the two girls.

He returned after a few minutes and said. "It is agreed, if he comes and asks for either of you he will be told that neither of you is available. If he wants to book and come back later we will not agree to that either. We will tell him there are other girls available who he can go with if he wishes. If he does not like that he can go elsewhere"

Sure enough, that night, about nine o'clock, Jack arrived. He had been drinking and was full of cheer and bad manners. He put fifty pounds down and said that he wanted a turn with Luscious Lizzie.

This was politely declined; he was told she was unavailable. He said he would take a turn with her friend, the other one with the baby. Again this was declined and instead he was offered his choice of the other ladies.

He said he wanted to make an appointment with Lizzie for the next night; he was told that also was not possible.

He asked, "How about an appointment with her friend?"

"Sorry sir, neither of these ladies is available for you."

He started to get mad, to bellow and shout. Lizzie faintly heard him downstairs. Then the two house men each took an elbow and moved him outside. He stood there for five minutes, shouting abuse, until a helpful local policeman suggested that he calm down.

Lizzie was told this when she took a break, an hour later, by Madam and Robbie. Madam said, with a half-smile, that she was pleased to see the back of him; she could gladly do without such a rude gentlemen in her establishment.

They all hoped this was the end of it, but Lizzie had a dread feeling inside, she sensed that this man was bad to the core, just like Evie had said and would not be stopped easily.

Two days passed and her anxiety faded. On the third day, a Thursday, as she and Becky were eating a late breakfast in the kitchen, Robbie came to see them, with an anxious look.

The first thing he asked Lizzie was how old she was. It was a question no one had asked since she had been here, with her thinned down body and face, from when she was sick and her baby, people assumed she was seventeen or eighteen.

Lizzie had a sinking feeling; her birthday was the end of November, in six weeks, when she would be sixteen, she said.

Robbie groaned and slapped his hand on his forehead. "Why did I not ask you this when I first met you, we could have found a place for you, doing house work. Then, when you were sixteen, in six more weeks, you could have started this work if you wanted," he said.

He said a social worker and a policeman had just come to the front of the house, talking to Madam. They told her they had reliable information that one of their girls, named Lizzie, was underage, and also had a baby.

Now they were asking to interview her. If it was found to be true she would be taken away and placed in a home for girls. Her baby would be placed into foster care while waiting for adoption. If it was true Madam's establishment would also be prosecuted for an underage person.

Robbie was almost sure that the source of the information was Jack Mackenzie. Lizzie nodded her head; she said her date of birth was written in the guest book at that house.

Lizzie shook her head in a daze, it was all true but why was life so unfair, she was only trying to make a life for herself and her daughter; she was not harming anyone.

She could feel tears pricking her eyes; she did not want to go away, not yet, not again, just when she felt safe and had found new friends, especially Robbie and Becky. Her friends both came and put their arms around her, feeding her support. After a minute she wiped her eyes and stood straight. "What do you think I should do?" she asked Robbie.

Robbie said he thought the best thing was for her to leave the premises and find another place to stay, in a different suburb not too close to here, where they would not know to look for her. Perhaps, in a couple months' time, when it all settled down, she could come back, as everyone here liked her and Madam did not want to lose her. But she could not stay here now; it would only cause trouble for everyone.

He said that for now Madam had sent the social worker and policeman away. She told them that she did not believe their accusations, but they could come back later to ask Lizzie directly. She said Lizzie had gone shopping, but she expected she would be back later that afternoon.

If Lizzie was not there when they came back, then Rebecca could just say her friend had been called away to see her mother in Sydney and she was not sure when she would return. Without Lizzie here anymore no one would have any case, there was nothing to prove it was true, it was just idle gossip. Then Madam could find a way to settle it down, she knew a person or two in higher places. But that would not work if the real Lizzie and baby were here and her age was confirmed.

Robbie handed Lizzie a hundred pounds, this was from him and Madam to help for now and if she wrote with an address they would help with some more if needed. She took the money and thanked him, tears in her eyes.

He held out his arms and hugged her so tight. "I will miss you so much, I hate to say goodbye; you will always be most special to me. Please write to me when you have another home and tell me where you are. Wherever it is, I will come and see you there."

Lizzie stared dumbly at him; she could not promise what she could not undertake to give. But he stood there, lifted her face, and made her look at him. Finally she gave her promise, and she knew she must find a way to keep it.

Of all the people here, the one she most would miss was this man, she wanted so much for him to say that he would come with her, that he would take care of her. In her misery she realised that what she felt for this man, was much more than friendship, and she wanted to be able to say this to him, and find a way to stay with him. But this time and those choices were gone. So, having given her promise, she turned and walked away without looking back.

Now it was only her and Becky. She packed what she could carry in a light bag, and Becky gave Lizzie her own pram, it was much better than Lizzie's old and battered one, and had a place behind and underneath to carry her things.

They held each other tight for a minute more and both cried a bit. Then Becky led her out to the back gate. It led to a lane which came out into the street behind. They walked together to this street then they hugged again.

Lizzie looked out both ways, no one was in sight. Rebecca still held her hand. Lizzie looked at her friend, and with all the strength she could muster, she said.

"I must go away again, I am not sure where, but it will be far away. I will write and tell you where once I am able. Promise me that one day, perhaps when you meet someone that you really like, you will come away from here too. I know this place is good for now, but one day you must make your own life, with your child, somewhere else."

Becky nodded, "I know that too and I promise it. A time will come, soon, when this is not the right place for a small child. I had hoped that you and I could do this together, like sisters. But we will both have to do it on our own now. I just wish I was as strong as you are."

Lizzie gave Becky's hand a final squeeze and walked away. She made herself not look back.

Chapter 11 - Escape West

Lizzie had no clear plan in mind, but she had already made up her mind she must leave Melbourne. She did not want to take the risk that these people would find her and Catherine somewhere else; next time she may not be so lucky and get advanced warning.

So she found her way to the tram stop and headed for the city, thinking as she went. It was past time for aimless flight, she had enough money, more than four hundred pounds. It would last her for a good while and she must use it well, to get to a place of security for both her and Catherine, where she could stay and watch her child grow. Both she and her child needed a place to call their own, somewhere they came home to each night, with friends around, and which no one would try to take away from them.

While she could not be certain, and would return to it if needed, she also thought her time as a prostitute was over. She did not want to undo this time, she had learned so much about herself and about many other parts of life in the doing. But now she had a choice again and her mind was clear; yes, she would choose another life.

She had a half formed idea to head west, at least to Adelaide and maybe further. She thought there was a Trans Australian Railway which ran all the way across the country to Perth in Western Australia. So maybe she would head for there. Now that the tram was taking her to the city she decided that her first destination was Spencer Street Railway Station. That was where her Sydney train had come to and she thought that other trains out of Melbourne would leave from there.

Once she was there she would find out how to catch a train west. Now the plan was clear; she would go first to Adelaide, maybe stop there for a night and then head on at least until she came to Perth, maybe even further. She pictured a map of Australia in her head, and imagined the furthest away part of Western Australia, names like the Kimberley and Broome sprang to mind, that was it, Broome sounded right, a B name like Balmain, but so far away that the chance of anyone finding her there was vanishingly small.

Once at the station the ticket man told her that she should take a train to Adelaide and then catch a further train on from there. The next train departed this evening about eight o'clock and arrived there mid-morning tomorrow. So she bought a ticket to Adelaide, it was about the same cost as one to Sydney. She could have bought a ticket for the whole journey to Perth, but she preferred the idea of stopping for a day or two in Adelaide, she had never been there and had only read small amounts about it in books at school. So she liked the idea of having a day there to rest and look around.

It would not eat into her savings much and she thought it would also be good for Catherine to break the trip. She could also buy things there for the longer trip, the man said it was another three or four days from there to Perth and, even though she could buy some food on the train and at the various stops, she sensed she needed to be better prepared for such a long trip. She was sure no one in Adelaide would be suspicious of her, so once she was gone from Melbourne she could take her time.

She now had about eight hours to pass until her train left so she decided that she would go and walk around Melbourne, she had not been back to the city since her arrival over three months before. She found it hard to believe it was so little time since she had arrived here; the girl expecting the baby who came that day seemed another person, from another distant life.

This was one part of her life that she was glad she would never have to relive it; yes there had been some good times, but overall it had been so hard, particularly in the time after Evie died and before moving in with Rebecca; the cold, no money, no food and no glimpse of a path to a future.

She was determined she would never regret her life at the brothel because of the freedom it had bought her.

After an hour of walking around and window shopping she saw a sign for a public library. She was ready to sit down and feed her baby. She thought this might be a good place. It was out of the weather and, even though well into spring, the day was cool with a gusty wind.

So she went inside and, after finding a quiet corner to feed Catherine, started to browse the bookshelves. She had barely read anything since her arrival in Melbourne and now that she was back in such a place she realised how much she had missed this part of her life, the gaining of knowledge and the filling of her imagination that went along with it.

She decided she would use this as a time to find out about the places she was going to. With the help of a librarian she located a book of Australian maps along with books about Adelaide, Perth and the Kimberley area of Western Australia, there was even one dedicated to the town of Broome. She spent two hours ravenously devouring all this information; it was such a joy to use her brain for discovery again.

Then, realising she had barely eaten today, just a few mouthfuls of breakfast, she decided that she would go and find a cafe for a hot lunch. As she left she saw a pile of books to one side. She asked the librarian about these, what were they?

"Oh, we are selling off surplus books that no one has read recently, just a shilling each." the librarian said. She selected and bought five, thinking one for each day of her trip. Even though they added to her luggage she was pleased. It seemed such an unexpected delight that, for her trip, in all those many hours to come when her baby slept, that she might have time to just sit and read. Right now she thought, *if there is a place called heaven this is near enough to it, free to live within her mind.*

The afternoon meandered away. Lizzie returned to the library to keep reading. By the time it was closing she felt she had absorbed most of what she could know from books about the places she was going. She knew lots about pearl diving, crocodiles, cyclones, sun-baked heat and desert; she also knew that she would have to go by road or boat from Perth to get to Broome. Which way she would choose she did not know; but she grasped that it was a very long way further, almost as far as getting to Perth from Melbourne. The books said the roads were really bad, so she thought a boat may be worth trying for.

About six o'clock, as dusk was falling, she returned to the railway station and ate a meal in its dining room before boarding. Now, suddenly, she felt anxious, she felt as if a sixth sense was telling her to be careful, that someone might come here looking for her. She knew the Sydney train was leaving soon and then the Adelaide train another half hour later. Imagine if the police and a social worker came here to try and intercept her before departure. She moved with her plate of food to the furthest corner of the dining room, next to the toilets and an outside exit. She would finish her meal here and not go outside until the train was due to board. For now she saw no one suspicious and decided that it must be due to her overactive imagination.

But still the anxiety sat inside her. She had gone through so much to get to this place; she would not be careless now. She decided she would find a hidden place and wait until the very last minute to board, just to make sure they were not checking the train. It was not past Jack to put others up to something like that.

Then, if she saw anyone who looked like an official waiting around, checking the passengers, or checking the carriages, she would find another way to travel or wait for another day, the ticket seller had told her another train left in the early morning. It was now a little over half an hour to her departure and they were about to open this train platform for boarding. She found a well hidden corner, next to a passage leading to the outside, but with a view of the platform entrance for her train. People were starting to gather there to queue and board, and a man was starting to open the gate, and check tickets.

Lizzie sat there with a clear view, but almost hidden. She was holding a newspaper up to cover her face, and her pram was hidden further out of sight behind her chair.

The hairs on her neck stood up, a policeman and Jack were standing there, talking together. They were both scrutinising the passengers that had gathered. Retreat was the order of the day; she would try again in the morning. The ticket office was around the corner out of sight of the platform entrance. She asked them to change her booking to the first train next morning, taking care not to let them sight her baby, perhaps her description with the child had been used as a way of trying to locate her.

The lady who served her was helpful and unsuspicious. "Sure love, I can do that, just a ten shilling fee for the rebooking. She took her new ticket and left the station, finding a nearby hotel for the night.

She returned for next morning's seven o'clock train, anxiety running through her. This time there was only a sleepy ticket seller and a handful of sleepy passengers. Still she waited until departure was in less than five minute before she plucked up her courage and quickly boarded. As the train rolled away she felt herself shaking with relief.

It was six days before she alighted in Perth, it had been a long and slow trip but now she was really starting to feel safe. From Adelaide she had treated herself to a sleeper, shared with an older lady. The two made occasional friendly conversation but mostly she read, slept and entertained her baby. Despite the long trip she felt well rested.

She found a boat to take her north, a coastal steamer. It was leaving in a week for a trip along the west coast to Darwin and return, stopping at all the main towns. She booked a passage to Broome. She stayed in a boarding house in Freemantle, near the docks, until it left. Time passed quickly; she found the people were friendly. Her baby led to many easy conversations and smiles.

While there she wrote a letter to Julie, telling her of her need to flee again, and also about her life in Melbourne. She decided to hide nothing, telling her about Evie and that life, telling her about working in the café and meeting Becky, and then when the other money ran out taking a job in the brothel, selling sex for money.

She said it was a hard choice but she was not ashamed, she had saved four hundred pounds and a chance for a new life which would not have come without this. But now she hoped to leave this street girl life behind her.

She even told about meeting this man, Robbie and the wonderful times they had together, and that she had told Robbie about the rape and how that had helped her. She even said that she thought she was in love with him, but now she must put him behind and get on with a life on her own, though she missed him so much. When she finished she felt it was good to have said all this, even if only to her friend.

She thought of writing a letter to Robbie, to try and say what she felt about him, in the hope he felt too, an attempt to keep part of her promise and at least tell him where she was going. Several times she wrote words and scratched them out, crumpling each sheet.

Finally she put her pen aside, tears misting her eyes. It was just too hard. He could have come with her, right then when she left, if he had really wanted. She was now determined to block him out of her mind, not to remember those nights when they had joined their bodies together and she had loved him with all her being. That had to be left behind, as a part of her childhood, her first discovery of love. Now she must move on.

So instead of Robbie she made herself think of her mother and her brother. Now she found the photos from Evie, the only pictures of her friend. She put two copies of the photos of her, Catherine and Evie into the envelope for Julie. She asked Julie to give one set to her mother, and to tell her about this lady who had helped her when the baby was born. Then the letter was posted.

After the week in Freemantle Lizzie was pleased when it was time to sail. This time she shared a small cabin with another lady, polite but less friendly. This trip was not as easy; often a strong wind was blowing, giving a heavy swell. She discovered sea-sickness, and at each town she thought of leaving the boat to avoid further travel. But something drove her on, slowly the trip progressed and the boat moved north into calmer waters.

A week later she was standing on dry land again, in hot sunshine. She was on a wharf in Broome, breathing in salty tropical air.

She still had three hundred and ten pounds. She was pleased, she had crossed to the furthest side of this country, she still had money to spare which should allow her to establish a life here and she had encountered no more difficulty than a little rough sea weather.

Chapter 12 - A New Start

Lizzie decided that she had to start her new life in the west with an outward appearance of confidence and prosperity.

She had bought a neat second hand bag in Perth for her clothes, and a couple of light but smart outfits, which better suited this weather She had also bought a cheap gold ring which now sat on her finger, an indication of a married status despite being on her own. She asked to be taken by the local taxi to a good quality hotel in the town.

Once there she decided she would settle in today, have her lunch in the hotel dining room with her baby on proud display, then wait to walk the streets of the town in the evening cool so as to familiarise herself and be seen about – a well-bred woman of means. Tomorrow she would start to enquire about the town and what it offered, both the chances for employment in better quality establishments and also the potential to start a business of her own. Before she could form a firm plan she needed an understanding of what enterprises were already in the town, and what opportunities existed. She would also look at other possibilities such as giving children's tuition using her own schooling knowledge.

From her experiences in Melbourne she had formed a view that, in most places, there was an opportunity for competent hard working people who lived frugally. She also knew that her education gave her opportunities for advancement. She thought that, if she managed her money carefully, it would allow at least six months before she had fully used it up. In that time she felt certain she could gain a new income. She had confidence in her ability to charm people with a smile and a polite turn of phrase. She had discovered an ability to read peoples desires and understand and meet their needs. She knew money flowed from this. She was particularly interested in a business that she could do from a house that she lived in. This would assist with caring for her child and reduce her overall expenses.

The next three days were spent visiting many businesses in the town, mostly asking polite questions of the local people but also giving small fragments of information about herself, that she was a Sydney girl, that her husband had died soon after her baby was born, that she had inherited a small parcel of money, not much but enough to live frugally, that she had felt his loss so keenly that she had decided to leave her home and come to the other side of Australia to make a new life there.

She wove facts and inventions together with skill, already she had job offers to work in three shops. She told these people that she would think carefully and seriously about the offers, but she first needed a few days to settle in, get her bearings and find a place to live.

She sensed that she was a minor sensation in this hot, sleepy little town. No one questioned her motivation; those who were born here seemed to be content in this place and considered it natural that others should want to live her too. Those who had come here from afar, like she, understood this was a land of opportunity where each had to make their own way. Some had stories of a past from another life that they chose to keep hidden, for others it was a step towards advancement and a future return to softer climes in the big cities of the south.

What set her apart was that, as a mother of a small child, she had made this move by herself. She sensed a level of admiration for this. By the second day of her inquiries she realised most people knew who she was and were exchanging their own stories about her, but this seemed to mostly lead to polite curiosity not distrust.

She learned that those who worked for the pearling luggers made good money, and that there were also a range of government employed workers who were relatively well off. In addition there was an obvious aboriginal population of mixed status, some station people who visited and other transient people who passed through the town.

All the eating establishments seemed to have a good custom, and the food was limited in type, of variable quality and expensive. In part this appeared due to limited fresh fruit and vegetables, but even more it seemed due to a lack of imagination by both the business owners and their patrons. With its ocean front position the town had access to high quality sea food, along with a ready supply of meat from surrounding stations. There also seemed to be Chinese market gardeners who grew fresh fruit and vegetables which seemed to be of high quality.

She had in mind both a business that served meals in the town and prepared good food that could be sold to the pearling luggers for their trips out, along with sales to stations and travellers who sought variety from otherwise monotonous diets.

Her mother's culinary skill came to her mind, making much from poor and limited ingredients; tasty stews, fresh salads and a range of dishes which utilised the wealth of the sea, along with a range of deserts which kept well in a hot climate. She also had in mind meals which could be frozen and reheated, suitable for stations, pearling luggers and people travelling out to work in remote places where good keeping and flavour after storage were important.

In Melbourne the other girls had introduced her to Italian and Greek culinary delights; pasta, spicy meat dishes, olives and dips. Most town people had refrigeration, as did the boats and station owners. So she had an idea if a business where they got to enjoy good food and all its flavours, served in her own restaurant, but could also buy similar food to take away and eat later at their convenience.

She knew any business had to be well located to capture the passing trade, but it also had to look inviting, both inside and out, particularly to town people, as repeat custom was the lifeblood of any business. She learnt from her last profession that those who left well satisfied mostly returned and they frequently recommended the services to others.

So she now started to look for an attractive cottage, with the makings of a good garden, something that could be brought to life with a little care, and which gave space to grow some fresh salads and vegetables for use. In addition a couple trees to provide shade from the hot sun and a verandah for casual dining seemed important. She thought, if she could rent something like that for a few months, then she could make it work.

Her ideal house had a functional kitchen, a room for her own living, a room for dining tables, and a display room for purchases, supplemented by a verandah that could serve for daytime use, serving tea and cakes as well as cold drinks and ices, and which adjoined a shady part of garden.

This was her image, now she must find and rent it. Then she must fit it out to serve its purpose. She hoped that, once the place was found, she would also have enough money to pay for some limited help, someone to serve as she cooked and who could also learn these same cooking skills.

To help her money stretch she decided to take a part time job, working each afternoon in a shop which sold pearls and other curios to the town and the passing trade. It was run by Elena, the wife of a pearl lugger captain. He was often away at sea and she had two small children, one of three years, and one of only one year. Elena managed her domestic life and the shop with another part time girl.

What Lizzie liked most was that she had a sense of kindred with Elena, only a few years older than her. She was also raising a family of small children largely on her own while her husband was at sea. She sensed they both had a hunger for advancement, and a high level of intelligence and interest in the wider world that set them apart.

She hoped they might become friends and each help the other as the years went by, she also knew that making contact through her with other pearlers was a good business move. Her only reservation was that she was yet to meet her husband, Alec, away at sea for over another week. However she could always leave this work if he proved unfriendly or difficult.

So she came there to work, beginning at lunch time each day. She minded the shop for the first hour while Elena finished preparing lunch and dinner for the day and fed her children. She watched the speed and efficiency with which Elena worked with awe.

Within an hour Elena, could prepare a lunch, feed two small children and have a dinner prepared to cook slowly over the afternoon. With her Greek hospitality she would always offer Lizzie a plate of food on arrival, which Lizzie would place below the counter and eat quickly at times when the shop was empty.

Broome town activity revolved around two main things heat and tides. The tides were massive, beyond anything that Lizzie had seem. At low tide vast mudflats filled the bay, at high tide the water rose thirty feet and came right up to the town, lapping at its edges.

There was a steady stream of arrivals and Broome seemed like an oasis to many of them. The heat in the inland drove people to this place, a few miles inland from the coast it was often well above one hundred degrees, with a hundred and ten not uncommon. Here it was generally in the nineties in the afternoon, hot, but bearable out of the sun. So people came from driving through the inland, heat blasted, and felt a huge relief to arrive in this town.

Broome sat on a peninsula which jutted out into the ocean. This gave it a cooling afternoon sea breeze, absent from inland. But now, as spring moved to summer the streets were baking hot to stand in once the sun was well up; someone joked you could fry an egg on the pavement to make your midday meal. People looked for shelter from the afternoon heat. Elena used this to draw custom.

A movement was beginning of long distance travellers, older people who wanted to see the whole of the country of their birth. They would pack up cars, utes, vans, sometimes Land Rovers, with camping gear and would come from Perth or the eastern states.

They would slowly work their way around the vast country, stopping at small towns along the way; a day or two each. Many saw Broome on the map, fourteen hundred miles above Perth, over half way to Darwin, as an obvious place to aim for. Broome was the start of the exotic Kimberley, place of strange fascination.

Few understood how far and how hard a trip it was on these bad roads to come here. So the people kept drifting through, many hoping to make it through to Darwin before the wet season cut the road.

The road south was said to be terrible. It was 400 miles to the next significant town of Port Hedland, in a region called the Pilbara. There was a small roadhouse half way to Hedland called Sandfire Flat. Otherwise there was no human habitation in these four hundred miles. This road was reputed as one of the worst in Australia, corrugations big enough to eat a regular car, which continued for hundreds of miles, patches of sand, and bulldust holes to bog and break the springs of the unwary vehicle. Many less well built cars limped into town badly damaged, shredded tyres, broken axles, springs or engines which had broken their mounting brackets. Some abandoned cars and trips and caught the boat home, some paid for expensive repairs before heading on, a few stayed.

Still they came. After surviving this ordeal many looked towards a day or two of well-earned rest in this place. With them came money and with money came opportunity.

Lizzie had heard people talk about the immense summer storms, lightning and torrential downpours, along with the regular cyclones that bore down on this coast. Most years they came from December to March and locals would talk about how peace returned to the town once the rains came. They also talked with awe and fear about the cyclones which ripped through this town.

Roeburn Bay, next to Broome, was protected from the worst by the headland jutting into the Indian Ocean on which Broome sat. It was the place where the original huge pearl shells were discovered. These formed the foundation of the town and it was now a site for a new cultured pearl industry. It was also where the boats could run to for shelter from these massive cyclones, storms with winds that ripped the land apart. Houses not well built were lucky to be still standing at the end of the wet.

Broome still had a dusty small town feel, but it was the largest town between Carnarvon and Darwin, over 3000 miles of coast. Other towns like Hedland with their iron ore deposits were fast catching up.

But Broome had its pearls and shell. For eighty years people had harvested these jewels from the sea. It began with the aborigines in the shallow water, then the Japanese divers in pearling luggers. Lizzie walked a row of almost one thousand graves that bore silent testimony to their contribution to this place; many were young men, dead from the bends.

The shop was often busy around lunch time as visitors came and strolled around the centre of town. People coming would visit the old town buildings, look at the boats, sometimes floating, sometimes lying on mudflats in port, and buy food.

An afternoon quiet time came for a couple hours, when the heat drove people into shade, and a sort of siesta took over. Many businesses closed for these hours and Elena tried to use this time to do bookwork and orders. However she avoided closing her doors at this time. With the heat came a steady trickle of people, mainly visitors, looking for things to do. Often she made her best daily sales at this sleepy time.

She had a ceiling fan in each room and this gave comfort while the rest of the town sweltered. She placed comfortable chairs on the verandah, to encourage people to rest in the shade. She used the windows facing the verandah as display cases. It gave the shop a welcoming feel and escaping from the heat of the bare streets brought them in. She offered all her visitors a glass of cold water, with a squeeze of lime if they desired. Often she would have tiny Greek delicacies sitting in a corner with an invitation to try. It was subtle but very persuasive marketing which gave Lizzie her own ideas.

In the first week that Lizzie worked here she used her mornings to look for her own business premises, but nothing came up that reasonably matched what she needed. She remained in the hotel, her wages just covered this, and she did not want to commit to a lease of a place until she found something to suit her business ideas. Plus she must maintain the appearance of the well to do for success to follow.

After a week of working there Lizzie sought Elena's advice on establishing her own business. She outlined her ideas. Elena was instantly enthusiastic.

"But off course, it is a great idea, I will help you look for a good place, our businesses can each help promote the other. Once you have a menu and a business sign I will place a copy here and encourage people to go and try it, you can have a display case in your sales area with small items and information on my shop and where it is. Perhaps I can teach you to cook my husband's and his boat crew's favourite Greek dishes. When they are in town I often cook meals for these men, give them the food like their Mamas made. So, when I don't wish to cook, I can send them to your place for some real Greek food."

Two days later they found a place that they both agreed was right. It was in the next street back from Elena's shop, but near the corner where the road turned as it came into the town. Its location meant a sign placed out the front could be seen from the road corner. It had a kitchen and three other good sized rooms, one could be Lizzie's bedroom, one a place for inside tables, one could be set up as a little shop for selling food and other items, and also serve as an office in which she did her books.

The room she selected for her bedroom had a door which opened to the back of the house, thus allowing her to come and go without walking through the business. The best feature was a large verandah which ran the length of the front of the house along with two large trees in the front garden which provided extensive shade to the house. This garden could also be used for outside chairs if she wished. The outhouse, which served as bathroom and laundry, was at the side of the house and separated the front and back areas. There was also a useful back yard with good sunshine. It could serve as a kitchen garden for vegetables and salads.

The house was an old timber house and very shabby, the garden was overgrown, the paint was peeling, and some floor boards needed fixing. But it was dry, the roof was sound, there was no evidence of termite damage. With a month of work, a coat of paint and minor repairs, it could be transformed into something of beauty.

Elena was already planning for a day of work when the crew returned to port. In return she and Lizzie would prepare a feast of the same food these men's Mamas would cook. To make it doubly attractive she would invite the single girls from around the town, the nurses and teachers who visited her shop looking for little gifts. This work would get the garden tidied and the house repainted at a minimal cost.

The former elderly owner had died a couple months previously. While initially the son in Perth was inclined to sell, he had found the offers, thus far, disappointing. So instead he had decided to rent it out for a period of time before deciding what to do. The rent asked was twenty five pounds a month, with a three month down payment and paid monthly in advance from there. A six month lease was required.

Elena even offered to lend Lizzie the money if she was short. Lizzie thanked her but said she had sufficient of her own to cover the first six months lease. But she particularly thanked Elena for her offer to solicit the crew's help for the initial tidy up and repainting. This would help conserve her limited funds and speed up business establishment.

So the next day she signed the lease papers, using Elena as her witness, and took the keys. It was so exciting and reassuring to have a place to call her own. She could picture it so clearly with its beauty restored, she and Elena sitting on the verandah, each of them sipping an icy cold drink as their children played below in the shade.

She spent an hour doing some quick tidying. Then she went looking for some basic furniture, something to allow her to move in and get started on the fix up, the choices were limited and the cost was more than she wanted, she decided she would ask around before she spent this money, so instead she went off early to work with Elena.

She found she was brimming to tell Elena about her plans and thought she might have better ideas about the furnishing.

As it was a quiet day Elena took out a pen, ruler and paper. Together they drew up a plan for a fit-out. Elena said Alec was very clever about these things; she would talk to him when his boat returned the next day. She also said she would not open the next day as she always closed on the days he returned to port to give him time and attention. Lizzie decided to use this day to get seriously to work on her new house, particularly to clean up the accumulation of rubbish and get it ready for painting.

She passed the next morning working there steadily, cleaning out the old kitchen, cleaning the stove, emptying old rubbish from mouldering cupboards, picking up dead branches and making piles in the garden; it was slow and physically hard.

It was starting to occur to her there was a lot more work to fixing this house than she had imagined and she was not hardened to working with her hands. By lunch she had several blisters and the heat was sapping her energy. She decided to rest in the shade for a while and to give Catherine some needed attention. She sat there, dispirited by the amount of work still before her, lost in dreamy remembrance of a soft life in Melbourne, sitting with Becky and babies in spring sunshine. She must write Becky a letter now she had a known address.

A toot of a horn roused her from her daydream. It was a ute with a powerfully built man driving. The passenger on the other side was part hidden by his bulk, then she recognised Elena's wave. She had brought her husband, Alec, to meet her new friend; he had come in on the early morning tide.

She instantly liked Alec. He was not much taller than Elena but built like a bull, broad shoulders and thick neck. She showed them around and watched as he assessed what was required with a quick eye. Elena made a comment here and there.

When this was finished he said, "Now you come to eat with us, we have a special lunch to celebrate my return and Elena's new friend. She tells me I must help you with the fix up before I go away again."

With this he slapped his hand on his forehead. "You know, I go away from Darwin with Elena because my mother is always saying what to do. Now I come to Broome and Elena is always saying what to do. So I go to sea and all the crew try and tell me what to do. It is my life, yes; many other people who all want to tell me what to do."

With this his face burst into a broad grin. "But for you, Elena tells me you are a good friend who helps her much. So I am happy to help you too. Tomorrow I will bring the crew for the day and maybe the next day as well. When this is done your house will be beautiful again."

She started to say. "I am not sure if I have enough money to pay for all these people."

But he waved her aside. "For Elena's friend, no payment. But once you have fixed it up, and learned how to cook Greek food, you can invite us all for a big Greek dinner."

Lizzie laughed and clapped her hands, this man's good humour was infectious, "But of course; what else does one do with ones friends, many dinners I think."

Chapter 13 - A Business Success

By the end of the second day the house was done. The floors were fixed, walls painted with fresh paint, another stove and new cupboards were in the kitchen, the weeds were removed from the yard and all the trees and bushes trimmed to give a semblance of neatness.

There were four tables and chairs with red checked tablecloths that someone had found, along with a bed, dresser and wardrobe in her room, all were donations said to have come from people who knew people who knew people. In the kitchen was a big assemblage of kitchen pots and implements that she could use to get her cooking started. The only thing lacking was a refrigerator and she had money to buy this herself, though she would not be surprised if one miraculously appeared, in the way that so many other things had.

She felt a huge sense a gratitude to this town and its kind people who had accepted her and taken her into their hearts. It made her feel she belonged here. Not that she could tell these people who she really was, but here everyone had a story.

As the work was finishing up she noticed one of the men from the boat crew working away with a tin of paint, doing some paintwork on an old school blackboard resting on an easel. This man was just completing his task, the words now appearing; "Lizzie's Luscious Little Luxuries", in cursive script with a pretty floral border. She looked at him with a raised eyebrow.

He laughed, "You can always change the name later, but our work is not complete without it having a name, so I did this."

The sign had creative flair, beautifully done; she rolled the words around her tongue. It was not what she would have thought of herself and "Luscious" evoked strong memory connections. But, what the hell, it was a part of the life that had brought her to this place. Plus the words seemed to work together, they flowed into a mental image which she liked, maker of things which gave others pleasure. So she would let it stay that way and see if it still fitted when the restaurant

114

opened. It could be distinctive enough to work, even if using her own name seemed a little vain.

Tonight was her last night in the hotel, and there was a party atmosphere. She went to the publican and said she wanted to pay for dinner for all her friends.

He laughed and said. "You must be joking. Tonight is our welcome to you, not often we get someone so new and fresh faced in this town, and someone with so much get up and go. So we have all decided that tonight is for you, to say you are part of our town now and we are glad you have come. This meal is on me."

Then, seeing her anxious look, as if she thought it was too much, he roared laughing. "It won't cost me, I will stand the dinner, but I will get my money back double over the bar, the crew are flush with wages from their trip away. They would already have spent them but for the fact that Alec told them they could not have a big blowout until your house was fixed. So that has redoubled their efforts to get it done today. Tonight they will make up for lost time."

It took another week until she was ready to open, and her first patrons were those who had helped to do the work. She tried to insist that they each did not pay. It was useless; getting them to take change from the five and ten pound notes they proffered was hard enough. However other guests were flowing in as well. Within another week, she had a girl helping. Within a month her staff had grown to three plus herself, albeit that two were part timers.

Her first worker, Ruby, was a part aboriginal girl with lovely honey coloured skin and a warm smile, Alice, a motherly figure, was her second employee and she soon had given her a full time job. Alice had raised her own children in Perth then, when they all left home; she had left her husband and worked as a cook in various places along the coast. She had just come to town herself, arriving in the same week that the restaurant opened. She was convinced this place would be a success; she said she knew if from her first glance, and wanted to be part of it. So she invited herself to help and said she was prepared to work for no wages until the money came in. The extra takings after her first week more than covered her wages. The third employee was a young Chinese man, Tom. His father was a market gardener on the edge of town. Soon he was bringing Asian greens to add to the menu.

It all happened so fast that Lizzie had a pang of concern that she had lost control of her own business before it had properly started. But it worked and they all worked well together. Mostly it was Alice in the kitchen, Tom and Ruby waiting on tables and Lizzie ensuring that the guests were happy and preparing a range of specialty dishes and sweet deserts; some of Greek origin that Elena taught, some taught by her mother in an earlier life.

Five years flew by. Now Lizzie had several thousand dollars in the bank. After a year she had enough money to buy the house that was the business premises, and the next year she bought the next house in the street. So she and Catherine now had a private place of their own. It also made space for more tables. Since then she had also bought a warehouse near the docks to store the various items she shipped in.

The business now had eight employees in Broome, and last year she had opened a second business with five employees in Derby. Its managers, Tom and Ruby, now had a child of their own. She knew she could trust them and one day they might buy her out. For now they shared the profits, each benefitting from the other.

The most profitable part of the business was the food supply part. It sold food to a wide range of other places around the district, stations, boats, travellers and the new surge of miners. She also ran a catering service for private functions; weddings, parties, business events, they were all good clients.

Lizzie tried to spend most of her time in the restaurant premises. She knew that her regular clients wanted to be able to say hello, and for new custom it was the first impression that most counted. Those who enjoyed a lovely meal with good service and her friendly banter were far more likely to return, even those who came only for a cup of tea or an iced drink on the verandah or in the shady garden, surprised her with their repeat business and the way they passed her name on to others.

She now had the grounds and garden looking lovely, beds of colourful plants and tropical flowers. She repainted the outside every year and kept the whole place spotlessly clean and tidy to create a good impression.

She remembered Madam's words, 'Our job is to provide good service to our customers, those who don't want to do so can move on.' She wrote these words on a sheet of cardboard which sat in a prominent place in the kitchen.

The only workers she sacked were those who were lazy or slovenly, and for first warning she would take them to these words again and ask them to read them back to her. Most took heed. On a second occurrence their wages would be made up and pinned to the sign, and they would be gone. If they challenged her she would say that they had their chance, now if they wanted to work that way they had they should go and find another place that liked their way better than she did.

She also told a couple who she thought had promise that once they grew up and learned the value of hard work they were welcome to apply for another job when one came up, after at least six months. In two cases she re-employed people. They now were great employees and thanked her for teaching them a good life lesson.

Her reputation grew as the business prospered, the diminutive lady with the lovely smile and the sharpest business brain in town. Some people at first thought she was a soft touch; few left a meeting with her still thinking that. She had a mixture of kindness and competence, she would readily donate to any charitable cause, but she always made sure her prices, while fair, left a margin to pay her staff well, and make a profit for the business. Again she remembered Madam's maxim, 'fair share for the owner, fair share for the business and fair share for the workers'. So while she would give discounts for volume, it was always based on the real cost. People said she had a brain like an adding machine in working out all her costs. She flatly refused to discount to undercut other town businesses. If others did so and customers asked her to match, she would smile sweetly and say to them, "Well if they are offering it at that price and that is all you can pay you should give them your custom." Few did, and never her loyal customers.

She used a brochure that Elena designed to help her promote the business. It had her photo on the front, along with a list of services offered and some indicative prices. Elena would hand it to all prospective clients that she encountered, and in the port there were many, boat owners, miners, goods importers, other business owners. Elena even posted it out to prospective clients in other states.

At first she would be surprised when people that she did not know would contact her, often just arriving at her restaurant and talking to her as if they knew her well. But she soon realised that Elena had hit on a wonderful marketing tool which worked, and as time went by she grew more comfortable with being a well known identity.

The town was growing strongly and there was plenty of business for all to share. Plus she was good to her employees. While she expected hard work she paid them well and favoured local employment, giving clear preference to those with a connection to the town, jobs which gave real opportunities for town's sons and daughters, across the full range of the different parts of the community, black, white, Chinese and other.

She realised that she was a subject of gossip and some minor envy, but she was determined to give back to this town which had given her a new and stable home.

Catherine was now at school, and her best friends were Elena's children, though she was forever bringing in new friends, gathered from all quarters. They all loved to come to this place; mostly it was for the sweets and ices that she served after school for those who visited. Often she would have five or six children lined up at the counter, each with an icy cold drink on the way home from school.

She gave each child their first one of the week free, and then after that she would offer them to school children for half price. Sometimes Catherine would pay for her friends with the pocket money she earned from doing jobs around the restaurant. She told Catherine, once at school, that she must pay too; determined she should know the value of money.

Her favourite nights were when all the boat crew was back in town. Then a special Greek feast was arranged and she and Elena would work together for an afternoon, helped by Alice and her staff, along with a tribe of kids, all wanting to sample the delicacies, particularly the sweet pastries.

Then nights would turn into occasions of wine and song, everyone laughing and dancing the traditional Greek dances as the record player kept the music going. They were all such good friends to her.

The only thing that perplexed others and she could not quite explain to herself was the way she avoided all deep contacts with men, most particularly unattached men. A succession tried to woo her; some in subtle and romantic ways, some more directly. She was never rude but found a way to put a distance, an ice shell that was impermeable. At times Elena tried to probe, but this was the one place in her life that she would not share with this best friend. A distant smile, a flick of her head, or a dismissive wave of her hand; now people seemed to accept her this way, most just let it be.

Sometimes in nights alone, particularly now Catherine rarely came to her bed, she would dream man dreams. But there was only one face that came to them, and when she woke he had retreated out of reach, leaving a feeling of faint regret and that most ethereal sense of Robbie's essence, now having become so distant that it only remained clear in dreams.

But in the daylight hours her life was busy, so she pushed thoughts of her other lives away. She had more than enough, her daughter was safe and happy with a tribe of friends and, even if Catherine did not have a father, she knew that her mother and a tribe of aunts loved her.

Chapter 14 – The Past Comes to Haunt

A couple weeks after Catherine turned six a man walked into Lizzie's café in Broome. It was early in the morning, just after eight o'clock. Catherine started school at eight, and Lizzie had just returned from the ten minute round walk to take her there. She left Catherine at the last corner, a hundred yards from the school gate. Catherine always wanted to walk the last bit with her friends, without grown-ups.

After coming back Lizzie made herself a cup of tea and a slice of toast. She set to finishing last night's tidying, resetting the tables for breakfasts and morning teas. Alice was tidying in the kitchen and a new girl called Lucy was due in at nine. She had this part of the restaurant to herself though the kitchen door was open. A knock on the door came, then without waiting for an answer, a tall man walked in. At first it was hard to make him out with the light behind him.

He clearly knew Lizzie. He said, "Well hello Lizzie, I wonder if you remember me? It is many years since I last saw you in Sydney."

She knew him at once, despite the years. This image was burnt into her brain. She could never forget him.

He went on to introduce himself, even though they both knew it was unnecessary. As if from a great distance, Lizzie watched as he went through an initial ritual of politeness. He said his name was Dan Ashcroft. He now was a manager for a Mr Martin Wallis, who she also knew. Mr Wallis had a firm, Newcastle Transport, which he had started as a spinoff from his father's shipping business. It provided transport and machinery supplies across Australia, beginning in New South Wales but in the last two years it had opened new offices across the rest of Australia, first in Melbourne and Brisbane, now here in the west, based in Perth.

He was in Broome because their firm supplied heavy machinery to the mining companies of the Kimberley. The firm was now establishing a Broome office which he would run. He smiled a broad smile, like he felt that he was a long lost friend who she should welcome.

He said that, before he had come to Broome, he had seen her face in a brochure that had been sent to him, when based in Sydney, as part of a package of information about other services in this town. The Department of Regional Development sent to this information to all prospective businesses who wanted to open an office here.

He had recognised her instantly. He had also shown it to his other good friends Martin and Will to trigger their pleasant memories of having known her very closely in the distant past.

Lizzie tried to keep her face bland and show nothing, though her insides were churning. Alice, who sensed Lizzie was busy, stayed in the kitchen and now closed the door. Seeing this some of her visitor's politeness slid away, though a veneer of snake like charm stayed.

He continued, "It is nice to be able to talk in private. In fact Martin and your other good friend Will are both to be in town next week and they also are looking forward, so much, to renewing this very close acquaintance with you. It is such a long time since that night at Nielsen Park when we all enjoyed your company so much, much too long ago.

"But," and he paused significantly, "the thing we really thought you should know, the real icing on the cake is that we have a new business partner, one Jack Mackenzie, who operates the Melbourne office of our business. He was visiting our Sydney office at the time when I showed Martin the brochure with your picture.

"When Jack saw this picture you should have seen his face. I swear he got quite excited. He looked at your brochure and said, 'Well I be; Little Lizzie has shown her face once more. What a delightful thing she is. I had the pleasure of knowing her in Melbourne when she was a prostitute in St Kilda; she had a little baby then, so I was obviously not the first to taste her charms, Luscious Lizzie they called her.

'But then, one day, she vanished. No one knew where she had gone. Pity because Social Security had issued an order for her baby's adoption. I thought this might give the brat half a chance of a decent life. But she was gone and no one could find her, despite best endeavours. I even wrote to Lizzie's mother, whose address I had, outlining my concerns for her daughter and granddaughter's welfare in a house of ill repute, but she never replied.

'So now she has turned up on the other side of the country, just where we want to start our new office. How about I come along, with you all, to your Broome office's opening next month? We will all enjoy reacquainting ourselves with Luscious Lizzie. I, for one, can't wait.'

Dan continued. "So, as a result of Jack knowing you too, we changed our plans. Initially it was just to be me and Martin hosting next week's opening. Instead, now, all of four of us will come to town, particularly to meet our long lost friend. We will all come here to meet you by yourself next Tuesday, the night after the others arrive and the day before our grand office opening party.

"I promise you, we will make it a night to remember for us all, you especially. Not only will we get the chance to sample Lizzies Luscious Luxuries but we are all looking forward, even more, to sampling Luscious Lizzie herself. I promise you will have an even better night than the one you enjoyed with us in the park all those years ago. This time it will be shared between you and four of us not three.

"Today's visit is just a courtesy call. I just wanted to ensure you are expecting us and are available. If you like I will make a reservation for our future pleasure. I am happy to book a table for the evening or, if you prefer, we can make a booking for your exclusive services for the whole night, if you prefer a formal arrangement. In fact, now we are all well-off business men we are happy to you pay well for these services, knowing that this is the way you now do business; money paid for services rendered. Or we can just turn up if you prefer?"

With a parting wave, he walked out the door. Half way out he paused. "Don't think about running away again, or trying some other lame excuse. Before I came here I called to your daughter's school, classes were about to start. Very trusting they are here.

"I told the teachers that I knew you from Sydney, I had just arrived and had yet to get a chance to meet you, but was seeking directions. They introduced me to your lovely daughter, such a sweet little girl, called Catherine. She told me exactly where to come. I would really hate for her and all her friends to find out about your life in Melbourne or, even worse, for something to happen to your delightful child. I hear small towns can be dangerous places." He was gone.

Lizzie had not opened her mouth, but she knew her carefully built life had just come apart. At first, when she recognised him, she had felt terror for her own life, along with rising shame and humiliation for what they had done to her.

But, when he threatened her daughter, a burning rage grew alongside this. For herself she could bear this shame, but the threat made to her daughter's life was different.

She knew that Elena's Alec kept a gun and she knew where it was. She had never shot a gun, but had seen others do so and it looked easy. In her mind, in a place of flaming rage, she conceived a plan to get that gun and shoot him from behind as he walked down the street, waiting until night fell and no one could see her.

But then, as her rational brain regained control, she knew it was futile. On next week's aeroplane came these other three men. Killing one was not enough. The others would know it was her, they knew exactly what Dan's intentions were, not that they would admit their role or motives. So, even if she escaped their attentions or vengeance, she would end up spending her life in gaol, losing her child regardless. Then her daughter, as well, would be at the mercy of these people.

She tried to think of other choices. Could she tell Elena or other friends? They might believe her, but for the story to make sense she would have to tell all. The telling would spread the shame to Catherine, living in this small town, her mother a whore, she a bastard.

They all believed she had a dead husband and a legitimate child. She had often thought of inviting her mother to visit, but knew, if she did this, the lie could not be sustained. So, over her years in Broome, while she sent her mother money and occasional letters, she refrained from giving her details of where she lived and what she did. She did this to avoid her mother making direct contact lest, in doing so, Lizzie's secret would out.

Now she knew, despite her attempts to keep it secret, the story of her real life in Melbourne had been passed to her mother. No wonder those occasional letters from her mother had been guarded and less than warm; she had thought the reserve came from her running away rather than trusting in her mother to help. Perhaps it was also that her mother trying to protect her.

But until now this town had believed her to be a respectable woman, someone who could hold her head high. And now this man was promising to tell all about this other life, shout it from the rooftops, or worse still, to hurt her girl if she did not give him what he wanted. She knew she could not live with herself if she gave in to them and gave them her body, but she could not fight them either, not in this small town. All these thoughts passed through her head in a minute while she stood there, silent.

She looked around her; the world of this quiet town was unchanged. Alice continued to bustle in the kitchen. But her own world had just crumbled, she had nowhere to go and no other choices but to run again, to get into her car and drive away, taking her small and perplexed daughter with her, ripped from security and friendship yet again.

She could feel hopeless frustration welling up. Why did it always have to end this way? Why was she destined to have every precious friendship and every place of security torn away, what had she done to deserve this? She had fled from Sydney; she fled from Melbourne; now she must run away again, this time from here to who knows where.

She could feel her body and mind trembling inside, shaking with fatigue from this endless fighting, raging against man, raging at god, evil or whatever it was. It was all too hard. For just a second she sat down. She laid her head against the checked tablecloth. She could feel tears in her eyes and starting to flow down her cheeks. She could not do it anymore.

Should she just swallow her pride, accept her status as a fallen woman and let these men have their way and win? Her life would be easier. But that was no choice, not only would it destroy her from the inside, but where would it leave Catherine, living with her mother's status demeaned, the butt of schoolyard jokes.

So she must keep running, her only choice was to go somewhere even further away, where no one would seek her. She remembered, from a childhood story, that Jesus had gone to the desert; it was his last escape before they killed him. She sensed this was to become her last escape too.

So now, without delay, before this man returned or his friends came too, she must leave this town and drive away, a running coward, going to the desert because there was nowhere else she could think of where she and her daughter might be safe.

Chapter 15 – Running Away Yet Again

Lizzie's mind felt very muddled. This was not something she had planned for. She had a utility that she had learned to drive. But it was really just a delivery vehicle, to take her goods from place to place. It had a jerry can of fuel and another of water which Alec insisted she carry for her occasional trips to Derby or nearby stations, lest she break down on the road. But her driving experience was limited; she doubted she had driven five hundred miles outside of Broome town.

She had held off getting a driving license until the end of last year, because she did not want people to know her age and for a license she had to produce something to establish her age. First she had asked Alec for advice on a good reliable car she could use and he had suggested and sourced this one for her. Then he had given her several lessons until she had mastered the basic controls, clutch, changing gears and steering.

Then, when she turned twenty one at the end of last year, she had decided to act on it. A driver's license was something she needed for her business and the identity papers which went with it were needed for a range of other reasons, such as enrolling Catherine for school at the start of this year.

She had run her own business since barely sixteen. In this town, where everyone knew everyone; they had all assumed she was an adult, in her twenties, when she first came here. She had grown up very fast when she left home. By the time she came here she had a demeanour and confidence dealing with others that belied her years.

So when she first came her and stated her name and gave a former Sydney address in Balmain it was accepted without question or verification, it seemed unthinkable to others that a person with money, a child and a wedding ring was not who she said she was. And once she had rented a house in Broome this gave her a new legitimacy and an address to be used for all the transactions that followed without any more questions.

So, in the end, she had obtained a birth certificate directly herself; filling out forms and sending letters away to the registry of births deaths and marriages in New South Wales. Then, when the certificate came in the mail, a month after she sent the papers away, she picked a week when the regular policeman was away and a young replacement from Derby was doing his job. Not knowing her, he barely glanced at her license form, just ticking a box that confirmed he had sighted a birth certificate and inserting these details onto her license. Then she had driven him once around the block, to confirm she had the basic skills required.

So she had her own car and a license to drive it. She could take it where she wanted, though some of her gear changes and take offs were still jumpy. In reality she rarely left Broome, others who worked for her did the longer trips to outlying places. They seemed to like driving whereas, for her, it was an occasional necessity.

She knew there was a main road that continued on past the turnoff to Derby. It went on through Fitzroy Crossing to Halls Creek, and then continued to Katherine and Darwin. She also knew another road turned off it, somewhere near Halls Creek. It ran down into the desert, going all the way to Alice Springs.

Alice Springs was in the desert and the desert was to be her new refuge. So she had a destination to aim for. She knew almost nothing about this town except a man named Neville Shute had written about it in a book called, "A Town like Alice" which she had seen in the local library though she had not yet read it. But it was somewhere in the middle of Australia and there were deserts all around it. These deserts would be her last frontier; past there she could run no further.

Lizzie went to her bedroom and packed a few clothes for her and Catherine. Then she collected a couple blankets and put them in the car too. Her mind was jumping all over the place, her thoughts a jumble. She knew she should plan better, make proper arrangements, but it was hard to think clearly amidst the panic that kept bubbling into her mind.

In the end she went into the kitchen and told her longstanding friend, Alice, that she must go away for a few days. Lizzie asked her to keep running the restaurant, banking the money and paying the wages. Alice knew how to do this as well as she did. Lizzie trusted her.

Then she scribbled a short note for Elena and asked Alice to pass this on when she saw her.

She remembered she needed money. She kept one thousand dollars of spare money in a small safe in the office, so she went and took that out. That would give her money for petrol, food and other expenses until she got to Alice Springs. After that she could go to a bank to get more when she needed it.

Her final destination was the school. Here she met the principal, told him she had to take her daughter out of school for a few days because she needed to go away on a trip. She imagined that all these people thought she was attending to some urgent family business, catching the aeroplane to Perth, it flew out mid-morning.

Catherine was delighted to see her and seemed unperturbed to come away, babbling happily about her school friends. She thought a trip was something exciting that you did in adventures.

Without further thought or delay she drove out of town. When she came to the main road she turned towards Derby and Fitzroy Crossing. It was just after nine in the morning when she left. The sign read Fitzroy Crossing, 250 miles, She had never driven remotely that far but she felt she could do it, it was just a matter of keeping going at a steady pace.

In the end she made Fitzroy Crossing by three in the afternoon. By the time she bought petrol and some food for her and Catherine the day was getting well on. She considered stopping here for the night. But she had a half formed terror of being pursued. It drove her on. Catherine had got bored, hungry and grizzled in the later stages of the last leg, but after the food she was yawning. Now she might sleep.

So Lizzie pushed on. It was less than 200 miles now to Halls Creek, the next significant town, and she thought they might get there tonight. She decided that, if she got too tired, she and her daughter could cuddle together under the blankets and sleep on the seat in the front of the car.

In the end she just kept driving. Finally she saw the lights of the town at about eight in the evening. She realised that she had driven well over four hundred miles in this one day, probably as far as all her out of town driving before. It had not been too bad. Her arms ached from the heavy steering and the shaking of the car on the corrugated bits had seemed to go for ever. But Alec made sure the car was serviced and it had a good engine, so it kept going without any hesitation. She had gained a growing sense of confidence in her ability to drive anywhere as she drove along.

She got a room in the hotel and the owner cooked them a hot dinner. She had met him a couple times in Broome. Now he seemed like a friend in this company of strangers. He asked her what had brought her to this out of way place. Not wanting to reveal her destination in the desert she said that she was going on to Kununurra and Katherine, she was to meet other family members there, they were visiting the Northern Territory. It sounded reasonable and was suitably vague. People in these places accepted the need to make long trips driving on bad roads, so no more questions were asked.

That night she and her daughter both slept soundly. Next morning, after they had both eaten a good breakfast, she went to the garage. She asked the man to fill the fuel tank and also to check the petrol jerry can and top it up if needed. She saw that the man also checked her engine oil and radiator, and felt pleased that this was taken care of. For some reason she did not check the water, she just assumed this jerry can was full as she had never used any, and had once seen Alec check it and top it up.

She did not want to ask at the garage for directions as that would give her destination away. So far the signs had been good and obvious, so she thought she could just follow the signs to Alice Springs. Last night in the hotel she had talked to a man who had driven through from Alice Springs. He had told her about a fuel stop part way and said the road was not too bad. So she was confident that she had enough petrol, and that there was also a place where she could get something to eat and drink which was within a day's drive. As an afterthought she bought two packets of dry biscuits, one of crackers and one of wheatmeal, a packet of lollies and a block of cheese, along with a half gallon plastic bottle of water which she put in the cabin. This would give Catherine something if she was hungry and stop her grizzling too much as they drove.

She headed out, feeling better about herself than yesterday. She knew Alice Springs was between six and seven hundred miles away, not too much further than she had come from Broome. Lizzie was confident that two more days of steady driving would see her there.

Chapter 16 – Only the Desert Remains

Lizzie drove out of Halls Creek following signs for Kununurra and Katherine. After a few miles a sign came up for a turn to the right for Alice Springs. The sign said it was six hundred and fifty miles, much as expected. There was also a new looking sign, hand painted, saying "Fuel and Accommodation at Rabbit Flat, and a number which looked like 198 miles, though it was hard to read as someone had shot holes in it. That must be the place she was told of last night.

So Lizzie turned down this road. At first it was a good road. A couple times station roads turned off it, with signs pointing to them, one was named Gordon Downs. Lizzie drove on steadily. The road was getting much less travelled. She passed one car going the opposite way after she had come about twenty miles.

When her speedometer said she had come sixty miles from Halls Creek she came to a place where there were two roads and no signs. There was a big wide graded road running dead straight and heading off at an angle to the right and a smaller road which went straight ahead, but was not much more than a set of wheel tracks.

Lizzie was unsure but she thought that the main road must be the bigger one; the smaller road must just be a station road that had lost its sign. Both roads were obviously used but neither had signs of much recent use. So, after stopping at the junction for a minute, Lizzie turned onto the bigger road and drove along it looking for any signs or landmarks.

At first it ran over dry stony plains with short grass and a few cattle seen in the distance. Then it started to come into sand hills. Lizzie had driven another thirty miles by now. The road was definitely getting worse, now mainly sand. It seemed to be solid, but once or twice she felt the car sliding and the wheels spun a bit. She concentrated on driving carefully. Another twenty miles passed.

Now it was just endless low scrubby desert sand hills that the road crossed. It was really just a graded path between them which occasionally crossed a small ridge sometimes of gravel, sometimes of sand, once or twice there was something resembling a creek but with no sign of water anywhere and very few animals seemed to live in this desolate place.

She was watching her speedometer, so as to keep track of the distance. She realised she had followed this track for over fifty miles since the last major turnoff. A bigger rocky ridge was coming up in front of her, and she welcomed the relief that it gave to this dreary and monotonous landscape, even though the ridge was not really high. She changed down a gear as the car climbed this hill, hoping to see something significant from its crest. She decided that she would have a break at the top of this hill, and turned to the side of the road as they crested the rise.

Without thinking she turned off the car engine when she stopped. She got Catherine out to stretch their legs. They walked around for five minutes. The view was just endless sandy ridges, seeming to get bigger as they stretched towards a horizon in the south. She wondered if she was foolish heading into such a barren place, perhaps she should go back towards Halls Creek and then head for Darwin rather than take her chances in this endless desolation.

She was starting to regret her decision to come this way, there seemed to be a lot more cars on the main road to Kununurra and Katherine, and despite the corrugations that road was better. She had a growing anxiety that she had come a hundred miles south of Halls Creek into the heart of the desert and no one knew she was here. On reflection it seemed a foolish thing to do, and particularly to bring her six year old daughter.

That was it; she made up her mind to return. She would return the way she had come and, once she had refuelled at Halls Creek, she would go instead to Katherine and work out her way from there.

She turned the key in the ignition. Noting happened. Not a spinning of the motor, not a sound. She turned the key backwards and forwards a few times but still nothing. She got out and walked around for a minute, hoping whatever gremlin was stopping the car would go away. Then she tried again. Still nothing, the dashboard lights came on but no noise of an engine turning.

She knew that a car had a battery and the battery was needed to start the engine. Alec, as part of the limited introduction to cars he had given her, had shown her where the battery was and how to check and make sure it had water. She opened the bonnet and checked the battery. It looked like it should work, the leads were attached and the fluid level seemed right. That was the limit of her knowledge. She checked the headlights; they were bright so she suspected it was not the battery. There was nothing else she could see that would give her any clue to what the problem was, but her ignorance was vast.

But what should she do? There were a few trees on the ridge, so she could put a blanket under them, in the shade, where she and Catherine could sit. While their food was not abundant they had two packets of biscuits, and a block of cheese unopened. They still had some lollies though she and her daughter had been eating them this morning so they may be mostly gone. There was a jerry can of water in the back, though more than half the plastic bottle of water they had bought this morning had been drunk to wash down to lollies.

She had heard of people pushing cars to start them. As they were at the top of a hill she wondered if this was possible. She did not really know how to do it but had an idea, from watching a couple times, that one person sat in the car, put it in gear and let the clutch out, once it was rolling, and the others pushed to make it go fast enough. If she could get the car from the flat place on top to where the road ran down hill then this could be tried. She asked Catherine to help her. Together they tried to roll the car towards where the ground began to fall. With them both pushing they managed to move the car an inch. After that it would not budge; so much for that idea.

Lizzie realised she needed to get serious about this situation. It was early September and the days were getting warm though nights were cool. She did not know where this road led, but she had increasing doubt about it being the road through to Alice Springs, considering she had not sighted anyone since she had turned onto it this morning and that was almost three hours ago. She knew it did not have heavy traffic but she expected to see a couple other cars in half a day. This lack of traffic was what had motivated her decision to go back. But, without a car, they could not go back. Perhaps they could walk ten or twenty miles over a day or two with the water they could carry. But they could not walk more than 100 miles back to Halls Creek or even a bit more than fifty miles back to the last major turnoff.

She knew that people who broke down in the outback should stay with their vehicles. With a jerry can of water they should be OK for a week or so. She decided she must check this jerry can, this water was critical. She untied the rope that held both jerry cans in place and wriggled the petrol one out of the way.

She had an awful feeling, this water one moved around easily and the petrol one was heavy. She lifted it, it was really light. She turned it on its side and back, there was no sloshing. With an awful sinking feeling she opened it up and looked inside. It was bone dry. She held it upside down. Not a drop came out. She looked inside, holding the bottom up towards the sun. She saw a faint line where sunlight was coming through at the bottom. Looking carefully she could see a hairline crack running along the seam around the bottom edge.

She cursed herself for her stupidity. *Such a simple thing to check, even this morning, why did I not bother?*

Here she was a hundred miles into the desert with her six year old daughter. They had less than two pints of water between them. What had she done? If only she had not panicked, if only she had not run, if only she had planned properly.

She gazed across the vast expanse of sand dunes with a sinking heart. She could feel fear and desperation really rising. The chance of finding water in this landscape was remote, she had barely seen anything resembling a creek in this last hour and any water which flowed would just vanish into the sand.

Now she looked at the small rocky range on which they sat, perhaps it was twenty or thirty feet above the surrounding desert. When it rained the water would run off these rocks, there was some chance that there would be a pool or two around its edges somewhere. It was less than a kilometre long, the part that poked above the sand. This afternoon, when it was cooling and the sun was lower, they would follow their way around the edges and see if any water was to be found. It would only take an hour or two to walk around and look.

In the meantime they must sit in the shade and conserve what little water they had. She had this awful thought of them both slowly perishing in this wasteland, she could not bear the thought of her daughter left alone here to die on her own. Yet she could not bear the thought of watching her daughter die while she lived on. Well, they must carefully share what they had and hope someone came along this road soon.

She knew she must talk to Catherine, to explain and help her be strong and understand. So she sat down beside her and told her the story in simple terms, the whole story about how those men had hurt her and made the baby Catherine grow inside her, how she had run away to make sure nobody took her girl away from her, how she had lived in Melbourne and done things that other people would say were bad so that they would have money for food, how she had to run away again and come to their house in Broome. Then, how yesterday, one of these bad men had come back and threatened to hurt them both, and that was why she had left where they lived. And now how she made a terrible mistake in coming to this place, bringing Catherine with her, where they had broken down and had almost nothing left to drink.

Catherine looked at her with big wide eyes. When she finished she said. "It's alright Mummy, we are together. We will both be brave, no matter what happens. Then she wrapped her small arms around Lizzie's body, cuddled in tight against her and fell asleep.

Lizzie sat in the solitude, hugging and loving her daughter in return. She had come to know one thing with certainty from being alone here. She made a promise to herself, her sleeping daughter and to anyone else who could see or hear. It was that, if they survived, she would never again run from men like these again. She knew it was her duty, not just for herself, but for all the others who they had hurt and terrorised, to fight back against them.

When Catherine awoke they walked together around the sides of the hills. They searched for water, but they found only dry rocky hillsides. By the time they came back to the car it was getting too dark to see. Nothing resembling a pool or a soak in the sand had been found. They each drank a small mouthful of water and sucked a lolly while they watched the stars come out in the desert sky.

It was so huge, a beauty of desolation. Beyond them only the vast desert remained.

Chapter 17 - Sophie Returns

Next morning they woke in the cool. Their mouths were dry. Lizzie rationed another sip of water, in her case she pretended to drink, taking only enough to wet her lips. Catherine was unable to help herself. She drank almost half of the water left in one swallow. But Lizzie was glad it went to her daughter, not her. She knew they could only sit and wait, hoping that someone came. They were too far into the desert to walk.

The morning passed slowly. By lunch the thirst was much worse. She knew it was getting really hard for Catherine, brave as she was. When it seemed that the sun was about in the middle of the sky she gave her another little drink, again only wetting her own lips. Now only a dribble of water was left in the bottle, one more sip for Catherine.

Her mind was starting to wander and, in a way, it was a relief. At first she tried to sing songs and tell stories to Catherine. But it became too hard as their mouths got sticky with the dry saliva.

So she moved inside her head, back into the place of her own childhood, that time so long ago when all her life had seemed good and she was happy. Sophie's face drifted into her mind, but she could not see it clearly anymore. Since that time of the dream, when she had pushed her away it was like she could not talk directly to Sophie anymore, maybe it was a growing up thing, but her mind image of Sophie was blurred, like something seen through dirty glass.

But she remembered Sophie's mother, Maria, really clearly on that last day when she saw her. It came as a physical jolt: Maria gave her a thing on that day, a little package, and told her she must never lose it and, one day, when she really needed it, to open the package.

She remembered carefully sewing this small brown paper package inside the lining of her childhood purse. It had stayed there ever since. She kept this and other fragments of her childhood in a small tin box. She realised that she had brought this small box with her here.

It was the only repository of a childhood lost too early, it contained all her childhood curios, pictures of her father, mother and David, a note from her father when she was eight – just about the shopping but it had his writing on it. There were a few other things as well, she could not think of them all now. But she was sure the purse was still there, and yesterday, when she packed up to leave she had put the box of things in the bag she brought. She did not know why she had done this, despite her panic. But it was as if, no matter what happened, she needed to hold and keep some threads which joined her to this part of her life.

She stood up, she felt dizzy. Catherine had been lying with her head on her lap. Now she opened her eyes as she stood up and looked up at her in curious wonder. Lizzie found the bag and rummaged in it. There was the box; with hands shaking she fumbled it open.

The purse was still there, looking old and faded, the outer leather scuffed. She opened it and saw her childish sewing. She could feel something still inside the lining. She pulled the lining out and tore at a corner until it came away. There it was; a packet of worn and faded brown paper with a small lumpy object inside.

She came and sat back down beside Catherine, whatever it was they would share it together; hope must not be extinguished so as to keep them both brave.

She unwrapped the package, having no idea what it was. She felt disappointment when she saw only a small silver locket. It was heart shaped, about an inch long and a bit less wide. It hung on a fine silver chain, and on the back was written, Sophie, 1906. She realised that it had a clasp at one edge which opened. Inside was a photo of a small dark haired girl.

With a gasp she realised that this was Sophie, the Sophie of her childhood and dreams, only even smaller in this picture, she looked almost the same age as Catherine was now, though their hair and faces were different. This brought the image of the real Sophie sharp again in her mind, but with this image came a strange sort of bitterness.

When Sophie had asked for her help she had given it, without hesitation. But Sophie had never been able to help her in return. Sure, she had tried to warn her before that awful night, but it had not stopped what happened. So what use was Sophie's face and image when what they needed was water to drink. She closed the locket.

She could feel tears trying to form in her eyes, even though they were too dry. She brushed these away and sat up straight, looking at Catherine, determined to not let her daughter see her despair. She looked again at Catherine sitting next to her in the red dirt, such a brave little girl in her suffering, but how could this help?

Catherine was looking back at her with very solemn eyes. She put out her hand and spoke in a dry croaky voice, "Mummy what is that you are holding; can I have a look?"

She passed her the locket and Catherine opened it with great seriousness. Then a beatific smile lit her face. "It is my friend Sophie; sometimes she visits me in my dreams, and the night before we went away she told me not to worry if we had to go away, she would show me a safe way to go. She is trying to tell me what to do now."

Catherine closed the locket and lifted it over her own head, hanging it around her neck by its flimsy silver chain. She stood up, and took Lizzie's hand, "This way Mummy, Sophie is saying she wants us to come this way."

So Lizzie followed; her six year old's tiny hand in her own. They walked along the road for ten minutes. They came to a shallow depression in the road, like a gully between sandy ridges.

Now Catherine turned right and followed this depression, picking her way around clumps of spinifex. After a couple hundred yards it became a discernible dry creek bed and after a further couple hundred yards there was a low rocky ridge rising in front of them. The creek emerged from this rocky ridge and they could see more low rocky hills rising behind it, another fragment of an ancient mountain range poking its head just above the desert sand.

They followed the creek line through a gap in the first low hill. Behind it lay a depression a few yards across before the next hill rose behind it. In this depression lay a pool of water, a few feet across. Tracks at its edges showed it was the drinking place of many small animals.

So they drank and were refreshed. They filled up the water bottle they carried and took this water back to the car with them.

Each day they came back for more water. Between times they sat in the little shady place they had made, under trees next to their car. They told stories, sung songs and waited. Three days passed. They rationed the biscuits and cheese, now less than half a packet of dry biscuits remained.

Although hungry neither felt anxious, they knew that there was more to come. On the third day they heard a faint distant sound and looking north saw a plume of dust coming along the road. They heard a clattering and banging sound coming towards them along with the noise of a vehicle engine.

Chapter 18 – Rescue

Slowly the dust became a car carrying aboriginal people coming towards them. They waved and the car pulled to a stop.

The people got out and came over to them, showing little surprise to see them in this empty place. Their words of English were few but their smiles and chatter were happy.

They made space in their car. Lizzie and Catherine squeezed into spaces alongside these black bodies.

An hour and a further fifty miles of driving saw them at a small aboriginal settlement, an outstation it was called, on the northern edge of the Great Sandy Desert.

It was little more than a few buildings made of timber poles, each shelter was made of four poles sitting into the ground and lashed to them at head height with wire and twine was a platform on which leaves and grass had been placed to keep off the sun. These sat in a clear space between low sand hills with a small rocky hill rising at the back. At the base of the base of the hill was a hole in the sand into which a steady trickle of clear water flowed and where the birds of the desert came to drink at dawn and dusk.

These people seem to accept their presence without question; they fed them, they shared their houses. They hugged and played with Catherine and she played and ran with her brown skinned friends.

An old man called Clancy and his wife called Rachel seemed to have been given special responsibility to care for them, his English was better than most and he told them how long ago he had worked as a stockman for Lord Vesty on Wave Hill and he could ride wild horses better than most. So back then the white men had named him from Clancy of the Overflow. His wife was a senior woman for this tribe who he had married many years ago and now she had brought him and her family to this place she had known as a child.

Days passed, then weeks, they could all talk some common words now and she came to understand that they were living in a community of people who moved around the edges of these western deserts. She understood that these people had previously lived on cattle stations around here. They had then been forced out when they started to ask for land of their own.

Now some had come out here to a soak in the desert and had made their own camp, a home in a place which no one else wanted. The old people had known of this soak from centuries of living in the desert, and they had shown it to their children. Now those old people were gone but the children, grown old, still remembered this place and its stories. So they had brought their own children here to teach them about this land and its stories. Some of their families still lived around Halls Creek and on other cattle stations.

These people called their tribe the Djaru; someone had written it on a piece of paper and she now rolled the words around her tongue. They lived a simple life; apart from the bush shelters there were a couple more substantial timber buildings, one of which served as a secure food store, to keep out the bush animals, but that was all. There were occasional white visitors and once every couple weeks someone would drive to Halls Creek to buy food and other community necessities.

But for the most part they lived here in their own place, far from anywhere. They offered to drive Lizzie back to Halls Creek but she declined. On the next trip someone brought her car back. A lead had come off the starter motor, soon repaired by a bush mechanic. She knew she could leave now but she chose to stay. She gave them her car to use when they needed it. She also gave them the money she had brought with her, more than nine hundred dollars, telling them to buy food in town for her and anyone else who needed it.

She knew in time she would have to re-establish contact with the outside world, but she was happy in this simple place for now. Her daughter seemed completely happy with her new group of friends and this was good.

As time went by she started to realise she was needed here. It was not about what she could do to succeed in her own right, to acquire things to make her safe, happy, or even rich. It was that here were things she could do to contribute to the life of this band of people. They in return did things which she needed.

It was different kind of sharing than what she had known in the past, except towards her special friends, though she had experienced glimpses of it, such as when all the town kids had come home with Catherine and she had fed them all sweet pastries, but more important she had shared with them parts of her life's joy and experience, the first lick of an ice cream, the season's first mango.

But back there most giving was in an expectation of return, that if you helped someone that they in return would do something back for you, it was exchange. She remembered how she had made Catherine and her friends pay for things at her cafe, she had considered it teaching them the value of money. But here such a concept was foreign, if anyone needed food and another had it, it was given without reward or question.

Here sharing was what life was all about, integral to all parts of each day of living. You did the things for which you had skill or capability and others shared what you had or did as a matter of right; they in return did what they did and you shared it back. There was no counting in this giving.

Here she could see there was no teacher to teach the children how to read and write. There were eleven children between about five and fifteen who lived in this place. So Lizzie started to teach them, at first with no paper and no books. She used a stick and the things around her to teach; she pointed to a tree and drew a symbol of a tree in the dirt. They taught her their word and she tried to write the sound. Then alongside it she wrote her own word for the same thing and made everyone say it.

Each day she made them all learn ten new words and before long they all had a long list of words that they practised. Often the older people in the community came and joined in, and while this added to the fun and laughter she insisted that this was serious and they must do it properly. Then she started on counting, doing it the same way, but also using fingers, with ten people she could get to a hundred.

A month after their rescue, Catherine came to her one day and said. "Mummy, Sophie has been talking to me again. She has been telling me about the people you know and how they need you. Your own Mummy needs you, she has been sad for a long time since you went away, and she wants to see and know me too, and I want to see and know your brother David too. They still live in the house where you lived and where Sophie lived. You need to go back there and see them and bring me with you.

"The second person who needs you is Julie, she has been angry for a long time since that bad thing happened to you. You need to visit her too and show me to her. Then she will really understand how, from that bad thing they did to you, a good thing has come, and she will not be so angry inside. Her being angry is making it hard to be nice to other people, especially to men, as she hates them all for what happened to you.

"The third person who needs you is someone you have never told me about, a man called Robbie who you knew when you lived in Melbourne. When you left you promised him you would write to him. Instead you have done everything you can to put him out of your mind and not think about him. He had been sad for a long time since you went away. He needs you to help him come back to a good place and be happy again."

Lizzie marvelled at the wisdom of her child, she sensed her rescue, which brought her to this place, was not just a rescue from the desert, it was also the rescue of and from herself; finding what was good in herself and using it. It was also for helping her friends and family, who she had neglected for far too long, to find the good in themselves.

She knew her daughter was right, the time for running away was past. Now she must come back to her friends, give them her help and support and let them help her too, she must never run away again when trouble came.

She remembered her promise in the desert, how she must also do something to stop those bad men who had hurt her, not so much for herself, but she must use her own rescue and new strength to give this same gift of freedom to their other victims.

Chapter 19 – The Lost Years

Robbie lay in hospital, his lower body swathed in bandages. The last month was little more than a blur, he had no memory of being brought to Port Augusta Hospital, and then of his transfer, by airlift, to Royal Adelaide Hospital. He had vague memories of his whole body hurting, of people in white uniforms doing things to him, of him being wheeled on a trolley from place to place and of a period when his whole left leg felt like it was on fire.

And there was another image that kept flashing into his mind. It was of Lizzie, wheeling her baby away from the house in St Kilda and, straight after she vanished, realising, too late, he needed to go with her; him running desperately after her, glimpsing her turning the corner of the street, rushing to that corner only to see her retreating figure turning the next corner, always chasing but never catching. He knew it was a dream. It was so many years since he had seen the real person, but that ache of loss remained, always there as a sharp part of the jumble in his mind.

Then slowly the blurs coalesced into clear images, particularly an image of his mother sitting by his beside, holding his hand and saying, "You have been babbling about Lizzie when you were unconscious but there is no Lizzie here and I do not know her. Tell me how to find her so I can ask her to come here. You would not talk about her so much if she was not important."

Then his Mum continued, with tears in her eyes. "Oh Robbie, I am so glad to see you awake, looking at me like you know me and that parts of your body are starting to heal. But you need to be strong and brave, there is much yet to be mended.

"They told me your pelvis was broken, you had a ruptured spleen and liver. They thought they would lose you in the ambulance. And your leg is such a mess, broken in so many places. They have tried to put the bits back together, but they said it was like joining bits of confetti. They asked me for permission to amputate it but I said no, not unless you woke up and agreed, or it was putting your life at risk. So they have left it and tried to fix it, but almost no one thinks it will heal properly or that you will ever walk again.

Robbie took a deep breath and smiled. His mind was finally clear; he could feel the weeks of repressed anxiety flowing out of his mother. He knew, through vague memory fragments, that she had sat by his bed, day after day; coaxing him to eat, talking to him, encouraging him to heal his body and his mind.

Now he had his mind back. He surveyed his body and surroundings. He was no longer hooked up to lots of tubes the way he thought he had been, and most bandages were gone. His left leg was covered in a plaster cast that extended from his foot to his hip, with just toe tips visible. It hurt a small bit but really was not too bad when he lay still. His left arm was also in a bandage, and there were still some dressings on parts of his lower body. But it seemed that the main parts of him were still there and slowly he was getting better.

He looked at his mother and took her hand. He felt great gratitude for her presence and her support. "You can stop worrying now Mum, I am on the mend and I will get better from here. Most of the thanks for that lies with you. I don't remember much but I do remember you being here and helping me, day after day."

His Mum said to him, "I am so glad to have you back, the Robbie of so long ago. The last five years have been lost years for us both. You from whatever happened with that girl, Lizzie, the one you seem to be unable to forget, and doing more and more crazy things. Me, watching my only son fall apart, the drink, the anger, the reckless disregard for your own safety, and me by being powerless to do anything to help or protect you, but always waiting for that phone call to come where they would say they had found your dead body.

"Then the phone call did come. They said your motorbike had come around a corner on a dirt road in the Flinders Ranges. It was on the wrong side of the road, and you had gone under the back wheels of a truck. They said it would be probably too late, they doubted you would survive the first night in Port Augusta, while they tried to stabilise you, but if I came I should fly to Adelaide, where they would bring you if they could get your blood pressure high enough for you to survive the flight.

"So I came. Then they thought you would die on the evacuation plane to Adelaide, but they knew it was your only chance, getting you to big hospital where they could try and stop all the bleeding from your smashed liver and broken pelvis. For a week your life hung in the balance but gradually you started to mend.

"Then them telling me about the mess that used to be your leg, how it had gone under the truck wheels and now had gravel embedded, lots of skin missing and the two main bones smashed in so many places they could not see how to put it back together. The only good news was the blood was still circulating, and your foot was still pink and not really damaged.

"So I was determined not to let them cut it off. They took you to surgery again and again, three more times, and fixed it as best they could. Now they tell me it is full of wires and screws and if it heals it will be at a funny angle and an inch too short. But I am rambling. The doctor can tell you all this in his own good time"

She now sat straight and looked at him directly. "Robbie, I almost lost you and I will not let that happen again. You must tell me about Lizzie, the whole truth. While you were unconscious you must have said her name more than a hundred times. You need to find her, or at least to try, if you are to lay her ghost to rest. Perhaps I can help you. So now you must tell me what you know about her. I know you have mentioned her name once or twice before, a lady with a small baby in Melbourne, when you worked in St Kilda, but that is all."

So he told her the story he knew of Lizzie, the brave young girl who had come to Melbourne in order to have and keep her child, and how she had come to work with him, how he had held her body and loved her mind. Then that awful final day when they came to try and take her baby away, and that look of desperation and terror on her face as she had fled. How he had made her to promise to write but she never had, even now after more than five years.

How he had known within minutes that, in letting her go by herself, he had made a terrible mistake. How he had realised that all he wanted to do was to go with her and support her. He had asked Rebecca, her room-mate where she had gone, only to be told she left five minutes earlier, leaving by the back gate and pushing her baby in the pram.

How he searched the surrounding suburbs looking for her that afternoon and had gone to the train station that night, lest she try and catch a train to another city, Adelaide or Sydney, how he had seen the officials also checking the trains looking for her, and him knowing he needed to warn her lest she came, but then finding no sign, his only pleasure was that they could not find her either.

Then the first year when he had tried all the ideas he could think of to find her, asking anyone who she might know, going to Perth, Adelaide, Brisbane and Sydney, looking but finding no sign. Then slowly losing hope, the endless waiting, hoping for a letter which never came, his anger at himself for not taking the chance when he had it, he knew her feelings for him, she had told him she wanted his baby.

But in a strange way through the accident and his dreams of her he had found a kind of peace. He now had this sense that a time would come when she had need of him and then he would go to her. So now he would repair his body and wait until that time came.

His mother said she would do the little she could do; make inquiries with authorities to see if anyone had any contact details, perhaps someone had an address for her mother.

A month later, when she returned to Melbourne, she began her inquiries. She finally found someone who found the file which dealt with this girl. It recorded a complaint by a member of the public, one Jack Mackenzie. It recorded that an underage girl, Lizzie Renford, was working in a St Kilda brothel in October 1964, it recorded an order issued and the attempt to apprehend the girl and her baby, it had a copy of the letter that the authorities had written to her mother, Patricia Renford, in Balmain, Sydney, seeking to find her and the short reply that came back.

"I do not know where Lizzie is. If I did know I would not tell you."

So now she had a Sydney address and her mother's name. She thought of writing to Lizzie's mother, a polite 'mother to mother' kind of letter, saying her son knew Lizzie in Melbourne some years ago and was keen locate to her again. She contemplated saying more, she knew Lizzie's mother may be suspicious, after her past dealings with the child protection authorities and the role another man in Melbourne had played in these.

In the end she decided she must meet the mother face to face. She would talk to her as one woman to another, she trying to rescue her son. Perhaps Lizzie had met and married another man and contact with Robbie would be unwelcome, but far better to know.

She caught the train to Sydney and a bus to Balmain. Now she was standing in front of an old, shabby weatherboard house. She knocked and waited. Then she knocked again. This time heard movement inside. A woman of middle age, standing tall and straight, opened the door and said, "Hello, how can I help you?"

She answered, "I have come up from Melbourne in the hope I could talk to you. I was wondering if I could come inside and tell you about my son who knew your daughter in Melbourne five years ago, just after she had a baby. I am not from the authorities but at my son really needs to find out what happened to your daughter, Lizzie. I am hoping you will listen to my story then you can decide if you are able to help."

So the lady, Patsy, invited her in to sit down. She told the story as best she knew it, of Robbie meeting Lizzie with her little baby, how they had become close friends, both women understood what that meant. Then she told of her understanding that the authorities had sought to apprehend her and take her child, and how Lizzie had fled. She told of how her son had been searching for Lizzie for years, without success. Then she told of the accident and how Robbie had endlessly repeated Lizzie's name when unconscious. Now her son, Robert, was slowly getting better but still needed to know what had happened to Lizzie in order to move on following his accident.

By the end she knew Patsy trusted her and would help if she could; she nodded and she smiled encouragingly sometimes. Then Patsy went to a drawer and brought out a letter and a picture, a photo of Lizzie standing in front of a building which looked like a restaurant holding a small girl in her arms, perhaps two years old. "That is my last photo of Lizzie, taken almost three years ago holding her daughter Catherine, she shares my middle name, my granddaughter. It was taken in a town called Broome, somewhere in the north of Western Australia.

"Lizzie writes to me once or twice a year, she says that she works there in a restaurant and is slowly making some money. She hopes to visit me soon, and bring Catherine. I am sad to say that Lizzie and I are not very close, as shown by the fact that she went to Melbourne to have her baby. She blamed me, probably rightly, for the death of her father when she was a small girl.

"But I truly want her to be happy. If your son can help with that I would be so glad. My only address for her is Broome Post Office. I think she does not want me to know about when she worked as a prostitute in Melbourne, but of course the Victorian authorities could not wait to tell me that when they were looking for her. I, of course, did not help them.

"I am proud of my daughter for keeping her child and not ashamed for the choices she made. I just wish I could have been there to help her some more. I also want to see my grand-daughter. But Lizzie has always been fiercely independent, since a little girl, and I do not have the money to go looking for her myself. Perhaps I have also been too proud to just ask her to come home.

"So Lizzie and I also need to make our reconciliation and if Robbie can help bring my girl back I would be so happy. I do not know for sure that there is no other man in her life but think she would have told me if there was. However I think the best thing your son could do, once able, is go to Broome and seek her out. If he does I only ask that he tells her that her mother wants her and her daughter, Catherine, to come home to see me and David, my son."

As she was leaving the woman gave her the photo. "This is very precious to me, but it is much more important for your son to have, perhaps it may help him find her and bring her home."

Chapter 20 - Life's New Purpose

For Lizzie life in the desert rolled along in a way that had no boundaries. The sun came up and the sun went down, food was found and they gathered round. They talked, learned, sang and laughed. Sometimes old men and women talked and children listened. Some nights they danced in the dark, feet swirling in the dust, tap sticks keeping a rhythmic beat. Often, on hot lazy afternoons, they made things using the materials in the bush around them, a man carved a spear head from a hard stick, a woman made a basket from woven grass, another painted on a flattened sheet of bark a picture of dots and patterns capturing the movements of the desert. Twice big storms came and they sheltered and sung rain songs, once the rain came and the big drops splashed through their shelters. The other time it was dust and wind that tore through their flimsy shelters leaving them broken with pieces scattered; soon after they rebuilt them.

Twice they travelled to new places, once to a huge lake full of water. The men hunted ducks while the women collected roots. All feasted in the shade of papery barked trees. Next time they went to a pool in a dry river bed to hunt the kangaroos which came to drink. Lizzie sat in the shade with other dark skinned women while the children played. One told of a very bad place on this river where, long ago, white men killed many of her people, bodies thrown into a hole in the ground. Lizzie felt pain far greater than her own. She told her story. The women nodded, they understood and shared her pain too.

It was nearly two months until Lizzie saw another white person. It was a man who had come to see this newly established community and find out what services they needed. He offered to build houses and a store, bring a drilling rig and drill a bore. The people nodded and seemed to agree, but no one really seemed to care. The man went away feeling as if he had done a good thing. He would return in a month and he promised to bring Lizzie a pen and paper so she could write some letters. He said he would also look for a few children's books with simple words and pictures.

A month later, paper delivered, Lizzie wrote four letters and a month later again the man returned and collected them. It was summer and hot and the rain had come. So most roads were cut, no houses were built or bores drilled.

A further month later he brought three letters back, but one was missing. Lizzie quickly scratched out another letter and gave it to the man to take before he departed. A month later she had three more letters written to reply last month's letters from Elena, Julie and her Mum. This time one more letter came back to her.

The single letter read.

Dear Lizzie,

Of course I remember you and I am so glad you have made a new life for yourself.

Regarding Rebecca, she left here a year after you did. She met a lovely man who adored both her and her baby boy. He lived in a nice house in Hawthorn. She married him a year later and now has three more children.

I do not hear from her directly but meet occasional people who know her. I think she prefers to forget she lived here, and I understand.

Whether she wants to hear from you I do not know, but her address is 223 Burswood St, Hawthorn.

Of Robert I have heard nothing for several years. He only worked for us for a month after you left. I don't think he ever quite forgave himself for what happened to you. Perhaps he was much more attached to you than he admitted, but after you went away it was like a light in his life went out. He got morose and drank too much, and while he was still kind to the girls I knew he needed to go somewhere else to find himself again or whatever he had lost.

We remained friends and occasionally he would call and ring in the first year of two after he went. He always asked if I had heard from you.

However it is a long time since I have heard from him and I think this means he now lives in another place, far away, and sadly I do not know where.

However I have his mother's address if this is of any assistance, not a street number but it is a small town and someone should be able to find her if you sent it to the post office with a cover note. She is Mrs Edwina Davies of Hill St, Warburton.

Please give my best regards to your lovely daughter, Catherine. I am sure she has grown to be a delightful young lady.

If you ever find your way to Melbourne again it would be lovely if you could come and visit.

Kindest regards.

Lavinia Lawson

So Lizzie wrote a further letter straight away that the man took with him. It was short and to the point. She did not know how to write it any other way. It read.

Dear Mrs Davies,

I doubt that Robert has ever mentioned my name, however I knew him for a time in Melbourne in 1964 when we became good friends. When I had to leave unexpectedly he made me promise to write to him, and I regret to say I have neglected to do so until this time.

I have kindly been given your address by Mrs Lavinia Lawson of St Kilda, for whom we both worked in that year. She has suggested that you may be able to assist me in contacting him.

I would love to hear from him again. If you could send his address or pass this letter on to him I would be very appreciative.

Yours sincerely

Lizzie Renford

She placed it inside a second envelope addressed to Warburton Post Office asking assistance to pass this letter on to Edwina Davies who lived in Hill St. A month later she got a brief note from Mrs Davies.

Dear Lizzie,
Robbie has mentioned your name to me several times and despite the years that have passed I know he will be delighted hear from you. I have forwarded your letter and I am sure he will be in touch with you shortly.

I will leave him to tell you his news, you will find him changed but I hope this will not affect your friendship. He remembers you very fondly.

Edwina

A month went by and then another, while she continued to exchange letters with her mother, Elena and Julie. She heard nothing from Robbie. She thought of writing a longer letter to him and asking his mother to pass it on. But she knew that anything further was in his hands. Perhaps he had found someone else.

One day, in that mid afternoon time when people are sitting around and telling stories, before starting activities in the evening cool, a distant noise was heard approaching, something like a car but with a different and higher note.

One of the older men nodded. "Mightabe motabike." No one knew anyone with a motorbike so they continued to talk and listen as the sound increased. Now a cloud of dust was visible approaching from the north, and then it was there, a motorbike stopped bare yards away.

A man, wearing a helmet, with his body swaddled in leathers, climbed off. He walked towards them all. He had a visible limp; his left leg was twisted and moved in a funny way.

Lizzie realised this man was coming towards her, she just knew, and she knew him too. His helmet came off. Her legs took their own control, she found herself running towards him and flinging herself into his arms. "Whoa" he said, "balance not too good." He shuffled to support them both with his good leg.

Lizzie did not care, she could feel tears streaming down her face and she did not care about that either. It was Robbie; he had come for her, he had travelled here to be with her. She buried her face in his chest, she managed to say, mostly in sobs "I am so glad you came, I have wanted and needed you for so long and I am just so, so glad you are here."

He gave her his old smile, "And I am more than glad to see you too, though you picked the furthest, most desolate and most Godforsaken place to bring me to."

As the weeks and months went by Lizzie could not believe how rapturously happy she was, they both were. They owned almost nothing. They lived here on the edge of the desert and they were a family and beyond this they needed nothing. Catherine loved her new Dad, he called her Cathy and she called him Dad, which she knew he loved. She told him with pride how she had told her Mummy to find him, she had said that he needed her Mummy but really she knew that, even more, her Mummy needed him.

Robbie laughed and said "I think we both needed each other just as much, but thank you for your help."

Robbie was very handy; he had built them a house of bush timber and now was building a shelter for a school. He had also put up a tank so that they could pump water from the soak, and he had put in a wood fired water heater so they could all have a hot shower at least once a week. He also installed a Flying Doctor radio though as yet there was no airstrip nearby. Beyond that little changed in this place or in their lives.

Robbie also fixed up her car which he seemed to have taken as his by right. After a month they drove into Halls Creek and went shopping, just simple stuff, new clothes for her and Cathy and some food and presents for other clan members.

They also used the telephone. She first rang her Mum, then Elena and then Julie. After she had talked to each one she felt so emotional that she wanted to stop. But Robbie insisted she did not stop until she had talked to them all and Cathy had to say hello to each as well.

Then Robbie rang his own Mum and talked to her, saying, "Mum, I am so happy and glad I came. Now I want you to say hello to Lizzie, the lady I have loved from the day I met her and soon am going to marry."

With that introduction Lizzie was lost for words, but then this kind voice came down the line saying, "I have known since he first told me about you that you were the one. Then, when I got your letter, I knew it would be you for sure. Now I am so glad he has found you again, having lost you for so long. I know you will both be happy together."

There wasn't really much for Lizzie to say after that except that she was the lucky one. So she put Cathy on to say hello to her new Grandma, not that the marriage was formal yet but it felt the same, they were even making plans for another baby of their own, and Lizzie suspected one may come along very soon, there was no lack of trying.

Over these past months she had written and told her dear friends Elena and Julie, along with her mother, the full story about her life. Now Robbie had also become part of the story. She was determined to hide nothing important. Each time she wrote a letter Cathy had taken to writing her own news or a drawing to go in her letters, things like:

"Daddy building a windmill,

Mummy eating a snake, yuk! yuk!! Yuk!!!"

Lizzie felt surprise they were all even better friends and closer than when the year had started, but she had come to understand acceptance was part of the power of honesty.

She also got a letter back from Rebecca. It was a kind, polite letter, saying she was glad to hear from her, that Lizzie was braver than Rebecca felt she could be in telling others about her past life. She would really prefer that part of her own life was forgotten. She did invite Lizzie to visit if she came to Melbourne. She said she would like to see how Catherine had grown up and would like Lizzie to see Andrew, no longer the baby who played with Catherine, along with her two other children.

But Lizzie knew that any visit presupposed that the part of both their lives, when they became friends, was a closed subject. Perhaps she would visit, Becky was still her friend despite all, but she felt it would not have the strength of her other friendships.

Julie increasingly wrote her letters about the investigations she was pursuing, particularly into Newcastle Transport, Mr Martin Wallis and his friends, Mr Daniel Ashcroft and Mr William Brown. Julie had graduated with journalism and law degrees and she was now working for the Sydney Morning Herald.

She said she was gathering evidence to use against these men for stories in the newspapers and hopefully in a criminal prosecution. She asked Lizzie to write all her memories and experiences of these people down and post them to her, sparing nothing. She then asked Lizzie for permission to turn this information into affidavits which in due course Lizzie would swear were true.

While Lizzie had moved beyond vengeance she knew this was a necessary part of keeping her own promise and for the giving of justice to others. Robbie gave her total support, he said nothing she had done was any cause of shame, and he was happy to stand up and tell the world both that she was the best person he knew and that he loved her all the more for her courage.

One day a message came asking her to be in Halls Creek the next day. She and Cathy sat alongside Robbie as he drove the ute and several of her aboriginal clan sat on the back. The message was vague about why they were needed.

In the town the publican explained that an aeroplane was expected in the next hour. It was bringing a film crew including both a journalist and photographer from the Sydney Morning Herald and two lawyers from the NSW Public Prosecutors Office. He knew because they had booked rooms at his hotel for the tonight. They were to fly on to Broome tomorrow.

He did not know what it was about. But they had specifically asked to see Lizzie Renford so he had sent the message out to her over the Flying Doctor radio.

Robbie booked a room for them in the hotel as well, and a separate room next door for Cathy, which she loved.

Then he borrowed the publican's vehicle which had extra seats. They both drove to airport to collect any passengers that came. As they arrived a plane, a fast twin engine type, was on its final approach to land. A tall elegant lady with blond bleached hair stepped out first. Suddenly Lizzie realised this was Julie; she looked so grown up and sensationally elegant. Lizzie felt dowdy in her bush clothes. Julie spotted her, let out a scream of delight, and then they were dancing around like two school girls, giggling with excitement. Robbie and Julie also seemed to hit it off.

Julie joked, "He is way too good looking for you. I want to keep him all for myself."

Robbie replied, "Ah but you haven't seen her the way I have; this girl really knows how to keep a man happy. I travelled half way across the world to find her and now nothing will ever take me away."

Lizzie blushed, glad it was no worse.

Julie pulled out a sheet of paper. In front of all, standing beside the plane, she said. "It gives me great pleasure to present this certificate to Elizabeth Renford, Dux of Balmain High in the Intermediate Examination of 1963; sorry it has taken so long to get delivered."

Chapter 21 - Julie's Investigation

When Lizzie met Julie at school in the middle of 1964 and disappeared to have her baby Julie was left with an enduring sense of shame, with a hard edge of anger sitting behind it.

Her friend was one of those sparkling people who she found great company. Lizzie always thought of herself as Julie's poor cousin, and looked up to her glamorous friend, but for Julie the reality was much more the opposite.

She knew Lizzie was cleverer than she could be, and was also much more hard working. But she was not worldly wise the way that Julie was, she did not mix with boys nor did she have money for clothes or fashion. But she had such vitality: passion and commitment were at her core; she set herself to do things and did them. And, even though she was not classically beautiful, she had something, a real look. The pointy chin, slightly uneven teeth, dark hair framing dark challenging eyes that looked into your soul and gave you their total attention. And when she smiled it lit up her face so totally that you basked in its sun-like intensity.

But at the same time, there was an innocence and old fashioned naivety to Lizzie. Julie really loved her friend, loved doing things with her and, as she thought of it, expanding her friend's horizons. But Julie also sensed she had a special responsibility to be careful with Lizzie and her vulnerabilities, that deep hole from the early death of her father; her fraught and difficult relationship with her mother.

So she had been determined to show her a good time and help her have fun. But she realised now, looking back, that in doing so, a lot of it had been about advancing herself, showing off this charming and witty friend who had such an ability to captivate others.

In encouraging her friend to come out with her she had been reckless about protecting her and safeguarding her. She had pushed Lizzie to come to the beach that day as much to show the interesting circles she moved in to Carl and his friends, and thus advance her own status, as to provide an opportunity for Lizzie to experience something new and exciting.

And her almost forcing Lizzie to come to the party had been more of the same, plus a desire to try some sexual intimacy with Carl, in a place free of parental restraint, due to the cover that her friend could provide. In the end, despite Carl trying it on, she had said No! She decided she did not much like him anyway, rich but hollow was the way she now thought about him.

She had never trusted Martin, Will or Dan, but had just played along with their sexual innuendos and nasty jokes, as they were Carl's friends. She had never given serious consideration to the danger they might pose to Lizzie and what, with her friend's naivety and alcohol, such boys might seek to do to her in this condition.

Then, having brought her friend to the party, and having watched her become intoxicated, she should have gone and brought Lizzie into her circle, found her some water for her to drink. She should have given her cover from those creeps. Instead she had chosen to ignore what she saw while she played her own games. Then when Lizzie vanished, and these men returned with their self-satisfied smirks she had not really challenged their version of events, she had not gone looking for her friend that night.

At a minimum she should have caught a taxi and checked Lizzie was safe home. Then, when she found a devastated Lizzie the next day looking, for all the world, like the many other rape victims she had seen since, she had blocked out this awful possibility, instead choosing to feel hurt at her friend's rejection of her.

It was only months later, when she saw her friend's thin gaunt face, her swollen belly and her quiet desperation, that she had come to her senses. Then she had been filled with a combination of burning rage and deep shame. This had endured over the years undiminished.

She made a promise to herself, on that day, that she would both do all she could in the future to help her friend, on whatever terms that help was needed. And at the same time she would get even with those bastards.

That night she had written her own memory of everything that Lizzie had told her and signed and dated it, then asked another friend, who she trusted, to countersign and date it too. She did not ask her friend to read this record, but just to witness this writing had been done at this time and place. Even then her very limited knowledge of the law suggested a contemporaneous record may have value.

Previously her idea of a career had been to finish school, and get a job in fashion or something else glamorous, a lawyer or doctor was a possibility but it always had her at its centre with an elegant image.

After that she knew that her career would go down one of two paths, either as an investigative journalist who uncovered and brought to light stories such as what happened to Lizzie, or a prosecuting lawyer who sought to convict and jail these sorts of people, nasty abusive creeps.

She became focused on her studies to get top marks. Then she went to University doing a combined Arts-Law Degree, with a journalism major. At University she became an advocate for women's rights, protection against violence, protection of girls on campus, protection of street girls, rape support and counselling services. By the time she left University she had talked to innumerable rape and domestic violence victims. She was already starting to make her name with hard hitting articles in the University Magazine "Honi Soit" about women's rights.

One downside of her experience and passion was that she found herself very distrustful of men. Every story she heard amplified her belief that men were inherently bastards. Since that early relationship with Carl, which had not gone beyond some heavy petting, she had become totally distrustful of men and their motives. Many at University tried it on but she had such devastating repartee and withering scorn that most retreated from first encounters. For those who did not get the hint she turned nasty with complaints about harassment and more. She knew there were jokes about her sexuality, like "the butch bitch", but she did not care.

On graduation, at the age of 22, she had found herself with a job as an investigative reporter at the Sydney Morning Herald focusing on women's issues. Women were a large and growing part of the readership, bringing this desire for equality and liberation. She soon interviewed many leading edge feminists, both in Australia and internationally.

She crusaded against the idea that pregnant women should be obliged to leave work. Lizzie on that day standing before her seven months pregnant and having just had her employment terminated was her vision for this. She campaigned against forced adoption and lack of support for teenage pregnancy, the same Lizzie fleeing first to Melbourne and then on from there was burnt in her mind to motivate this. She campaigned for protection for street girls against violence, abuse and intimidation, Lizzie the call girl was her motivation for this.

She had not been surprised to receive Lizzie's letter as she sat waiting to catch the boat from Perth to Broome with her small baby. She now understood her need to become a prostitute and marvelled at her great courage in this awful time, it only fuelled Julie's own rage further. And her admiration for her friend grew as time went by, the higher the adversity the higher Lizzie climbed. She knew she would succeed in whatever she did, that was the nature of Lizzie's courage.

It came as no surprise when Lizzie wrote to her in early 1971, soon after as she begun as a journalist, telling her that she had fled yet again from these awful men, and had taken refuge in the desert, their arrogance and misogyny knew no bounds. Now when Lizzie told her of her intention to stop running and confront this evil, she knew her own time for action had come too.

Now she had a specific purpose and four names to follow. She set to work. She had used her lawyer training and knowledge from sitting in court hearing victim stories. She knew it would help her now put together an evidence trail for a newspaper story and perhaps a trial.

She was sure there were other victims. She must locate them, hear their stories, record their details then encourage them to testify.

Within a month she had a name, a Newcastle girl whose mother had worked in the head office of the Wallis shipping business in Newcastle. It had happened five years ago and, on hearing through the women's rights grapevine of Julie's investigation, the mother had come to Julie with her own suspicions.

Back then she was a mother of two children, a seventeen year old boy and a fourteen year old girl. She told an overly familiar story.

Her fourteen year old daughter, Miranda, had started to come to the office to help her on Saturdays sometimes. She was a beautiful girl whose body had matured; she was sweet and innocent about men.

Martin, who mostly worked Saturdays, had asked Miranda to start doing jobs for him, just odd little things, but he had paid her and she had been flattered by the attention of this good looking man in his twenties. He was now married to a local girl with a young child and a veneer of respectability. Dan and Will still worked in the firm and were often with Martin though their jobs were unclear.

Then the mother had to go to Sydney for a few days, leaving her daughter and son at home together. Since she had returned the daughter had never been the same, she flatly refused to go near the office, she stayed in her room and cried a lot, she was moody and bad tempered and had dropped out of school.

Now she was in Kings Cross, a nineteen year old prostitute, addicted to heroin. Her mother had tried to find out the reason; she had asked her daughter, but got just tears, door slamming and stony silences. She asked the son, but all he knew was something happened that Saturday, the day that Miranda normally went to work at the office. She had gone in that morning as usual, and he was out at the beach for the day with his mates. When he came home that night she was locked in her room and she had barely spoken to him since.

So the mother suspected something awful had happened to her daughter that Saturday, she had tried to make discrete inquiries, but could get nothing useful. But the word of her interest must have got around, because within a month the company dismissed her, despite having told her, just before, what a valuable employee she was. She had worked even harder after this thing had happened to Miranda, but they sacked her anyway.

It felt bad and it smelt bad. The mother knew something bad had happened which had destroyed her daughter's life. But the cause was only speculation.

So Julie had her lead, she found the girl in Kings Cross, now calling herself Mimi, looking half stoned and sitting in a gutter. She was resentful and distrustful of talking to Julie. The first time Julie tried to talk to her she told her to get lost. Then she just ignored her. But Julie kept coming back, day after day, week after week, trying to make friends with her.

One day Mimi did not tell her to go away or look the other way. Today she did not seem stoned and looked at Julie with something like friendly curiosity. "You are very persistent," Mimi said, "Why don't you tell me what you want?

So they went and sat together over an ice-cream in a café. After five minutes Julie said to Mimi, "Can I tell you a story?"

Mimi shrugged, feigning disinterest.

So she told her about her friend Lizzie and how Lizzie trusted her, then about the party, then the rape, then the baby, and now how Lizzie had got her life together but then the men had pursued her again. So now Julie was determined to pursue these men. "I want them to feel the fear they have dished out. One day I will go and say hello to them through the bars of Long Bay Jail, and know they can't hurt others" she said.

As she talked she watched the face opposite, at first it was mildly bored, but when she said the name Martin she had total attention. Then, when she described the beach rape, the tears trickled down Mimi's cheeks, and they kept coming with the baby and what

169

continued. When she talked about the men coming after Lizzie again she knew she had her; she was Witness Two.

Now the girl was nodding and talking, her tongue and mind freed from years of paralysis, "Yes, that's what they do, rotten scum, they still come to see me every time they come to Sydney, often they don't even pay, and I still have to give them what they forced on me as a little girl. It was bad enough, what happened when I was fourteen, but to keep having to relive it again and again, even now, it is like a horror story that never goes away.

So now Julie had sworn testimony from Mimi. She had managed to get her onto methadone and found her a part time job out of the game. It was very fragile but Mimi was holding it together, just.

The third girl was remarkably similar but this had happened only a few months earlier, this time in the Sydney office of Newcastle Transport. This girl, Alicia, who was then also fourteen was an office casual who did cleaning and tidying jobs, after school, at weekends and in school holidays. Her Mum was on a disability pension and Alicia needed the money to help support her family.

And this time there was a fourth player, a man named Jack Mackenzie, who had been there on a visit from Melbourne. The girl thought he knew what happened, and maybe had done it too, but at the time she had been blindfolded and had not seen his face, though she knew the other men were there, both from before it started and from their voices.

On a Saturday afternoon, when no one else was around, she had been called into Martin's office to tidy up. Will and Dan had been there. As she bent over to pick up the bin, one had put his hand up her skirt from behind. She had tried to push him away but then the other two had come and started to fondle and feel her too. At first she had tried to fight back but then they had put a cloth bag over her head, making it hard to breath and threatening to tie it up tight if she started to scream. Then she had felt them pull her dress up and take her panties off before they did it to her, the others laughing as each took a turn. She had also felt them push other things inside her, laughing all the while.

For her one of the worst things was, when they finished, that they had given her an envelope with five hundred dollars. They said it was to pay for services rendered, just so there were no hard feelings. Alicia had kept the money, her Mum needed things very badly because they were so poor, but now she felt both bought and abused. She knew it would be so much harder to try to say no next time when there was another envelope of desperately needed money on offer, and could see that soon they would take it whenever they wanted, without even bothering to pay as she would have no-where else to go.

Despite the anger and hurt Alicia had kept going there to work, she did not have any other job to go to and she knew her family could not get by without the money. A month later, this man Jack, who she thought was there that first time, came back on another visit.

That day he was laughing and joking with the others, and sometimes pointing to her, like he had seen what happened to her before and had enjoyed it. He had a folder sitting on his desk, and he left it there when he went out to lunch with the others. So she had opened the folder to see what was there. Everyone else was in the lunch room.

She saw a pile of photos, they were naked photos of herself from when it happened, some were close ups where the men had put things inside her, her head was covered but it was still clearly her, even down to a scar on her leg from when she cut it as a kid.

The photos also clearly showed the other three men, Martin, Dan and Will doing things to her and laughing as they did. There were none of Jack, but then he had the photos, he was probably the photographer. At the time the rape happened she did not know what to do, it had been her word against all these men, and she did not want to give back the money.

But now, maybe, there was some real evidence to nail them. She was terrified but really angry too. Most of all she wanted to get them and get even. She knew they were planning to do it again. There was talk of Jack coming again to visit next month; she had heard Dan say that they would have a party on the Saturday night at the office where they invited some good friends, while he gave her a sick grin and wink.

They had asked her to come in to the office on that next Saturday afternoon, when no one else was there, to make sure the office was really tidy for that evening, when the caterers would be coming to serve their guests. She knew they would be waiting for her, perhaps with another fat envelope of money.

Alicia said she was happy to let nothing happen until that weekend so long as she did not have to go in alone, she just did not want the money enough for that. She thought that they would probably have the photos there then to gloat over, so maybe someone could do a search and catch Jack with the photos or something similar.

Julie knew this was as near to a smoking gun as she would ever get, she had Witness Three and she had photo evidence to prove what the three men had done to this fourteen year old girl.

Her lawyer brain had charges of rape, carnal knowledge and indecent assault mapped out. Her journalist brain had a scoop planned for the day after a trial verdict giving the full story of these sexual predators and the way they abused peoples trust to get access to these under aged and vulnerable girls, then after they terrorised them into silence.

But she knew she still had much work to do to put it together into a brief of evidence, something strong enough to convince prosecutors to go forward and, in the end, ensure all these men received their rightful date with justice and got nailed.

Chapter 22 - Back to the Old Balmain House

Just before Christmas of 1971 a TAA Boeing 737 landed in Sydney. From the door stepped three people, a tall sun darkened man who walked with a limp, a woman wearing a soft floral dress, with short dark hair cut in a bob, who appeared to be about six months pregnant and a dark haired girl who looked about seven or eight.

Behind them came three aboriginal people, well dressed but with an awkward sense of the self-consciousness in these foreign clothes. Inside waiting for them was a veritable crowd.

As Lizzie, Robbie and Catherine walked into the terminal, flashbulbs were popping. Julie and her photographer friend were there. Then there was Lizzie's mum, older looking but still herself, and a teenage gangly kid, David, with quite a few of his father's mannerisms.

Others in the crowd included some of the gang from Broome, Alec and Elena with a tribe of children, Alice, Ruby, and Tom from the restaurant, and a few from pearl boat crew.

Then there was Robbie's Mum, Madam Lavinia, even Becky and her family had made an appearance. There was also a whole hotchpotch of people she knew from Balmain, neighbours, school friends, teachers, and some of her friends from the factory in Pyrmont.

They formed an honour guard of welcome. Julie had assiduously tracked them all down and arranged for this day, determined that Lizzie's return after nearly eight years away would be a whole of community and friends welcome home for this amazing lady, who she felt proud to call her friend

Julie was also doing a feature story on Lizzie which was called "Sophie's Story". Lizzie did not want her name or Catherine's name appearing directly, so they had decided that the by-line would give Sophie the credit. Lizzie was just referred to as "my friend".

The story started with "This is story of my dearest friend, and of her own childhood friend, Sophie. Yesterday her family and friends gathered at Sydney airport to welcome my friend home after eight years of living in the furthest desert of Western Australia. Tomorrow she marries her true love Robbie. She first met him in Melbourne, but then he lost her when she ran away to protect her child from being taken. Lizzie was then only fifteen. It took more than five years of searching before Robbie found her at the furthest side of the country and it only happened with the help of her childhood friend Sophie, so this is Sophie's Story too. It is also the story of my friend's six year old daughter who led them to safety."

It was mostly a story about her rescue in the desert and a love story about her finding her true love, Robbie, who she has returned to marry. Lizzie was concerned it was a bit soppy, but Julie insisted that her readers would love it. And it would introduce her friend for what she hoped would be a much more significant feature article, after the rape case came to trial and some real details could be released. It was Julie' hope that the way her friend had triumphed through adversity would give courage to other victims to also come forward.

It did not go into the all the details of her earlier life, apart from the baby, but said she had gone to live in Broome after having her baby in Melbourne, to ensure that she was not forced to give her child up for adoption. There she had been driving in the desert and had got lost. She would have died of thirst, if not for a childhood friend, Sophie who had lived in the same room in her Balmain House half a century earlier. When they were desperately thirsty in the desert Sophie had come to her daughter in a dream and guided them to water. Then three days later people from the local aboriginal tribe had found her and her daughter and adopted her into the tribe. Then to make the whole story complete, the man who had met her and fallen in love with her in Melbourne, just after her baby was born had tracked her down and crossed the country on his motorbike to find her, smashed leg notwithstanding. So now they had returned to the family home to get married. They would first have a Christian ceremony in the church followed by an aboriginal ceremony, standing next to the harbour where desert sand and ocean water would mingle. Tonight her friend would stay in Sophie's room once again.

The following day the story ran as planned. Reader interest was huge, but who was this amazing mystery woman?

After a first night welcome home dinner with all their extended families and friends, tonight Lizzie, Robbie and Cathy were staying with her mother and brother in the old Balmain House. Lizzie and Robbie were sharing her childhood room, along with their soon to be born child. Cathy had a bunk in the attic, at the other end from David. She wasn't quite sure about sleeping in the same room as a boy but it was only for a night.

Lizzie and Robbie lay together, arms around each other and talked late into the night. They wondered if Sophie could hear them. They both felt so lucky and grateful to this child of fifty years past for their new lives together. Tomorrow they would be married.

It felt like a dream. In a way it was a dream, like that first dream. It was something they had both dreamed of over and over in years of nights alone, but it was real.

Tomorrow they would formalise it, making their pledges both in the church of Lizzie's childhood and down at Birchgrove Point, where Clancy and Rachel, the senior custodians of their desert tribe, would stand alongside a Garigal man from the local aboriginal tribe, an old man who held the stories and memories of this place.

They would mix desert sand and harbour water, sprinkling both over the couple to symbolise the connection of these two places, bringing together desert ancestor spirits and those from the waters of Sydney harbour, together to give a joint blessing from their many friends who came from both places.

Chapter 23 – The Court Case

Almost two further years passed, Lizzie and Robbie returned to their life in the west. Now they divided their time between Broome and the desert. The business in Broome was booming, but the desert was their true love and they spent at least half of each year there.

Now there were two more children, a rising two year old cheeky boy, Stephen, with tousled blond hair, and another dark haired girl, Sarah, little more than a baby, colours like Cathy and Lizzie but with a face full of Robbie, his mischievous grin. Now Cathy spent the school terms in town, she was good with her lessons, smart just like her Mum, Robbie said. But she came back to the desert on her holidays and she loved it still, speaking a fluent mixture of two languages and with favourite pastimes of digging yams and hunting goannas.

Then one day the call came. The court case was set down for next Monday, a week away. There had been so many delays and adjournments over the last two years that it was impossible to believe it would ever come to trial. But now it had. It involved a prosecution for rape for three men, each on three separate rape charges. And a fourth man who had aided and abetted in the concealment of evidence after the fact was charged as an accessory to one count of rape, along with upcoming charges for other sexual crimes in Melbourne.

Lizzie marvelled at the courage of the other two women, both having agreed to attend and give their evidence as well. It had been hard enough for her, but she known Julie all her life and trusted her. And now, with Robbie in her corner, she knew she could do whatever it took. But these girls' lives were still a mess, neither had really got over this experience and dragging it all up through court would be very hard for them, she knew how dirty the barristers doing the cross examination would play, and wished she could do more to help them.

But the die was cast and on Monday it would begin.

In Sydney Julie sat thinking about the momentous last three years of her life, that bright day of Lizzie's wedding and the tremendous public sympathy it generated; but also all those hard years before and after, with many times when she felt the threads holding all these cases together would unravel into an unusable tangle.

It had not worked out quite as planned but in the end they had Alicia's testimony along with Lizzie's and Mimi's, plus they had a copy of the photos as evidence for what had happened. These were found in Jack's possession, following a Victorian search warrant looking for child pornography, at his house in Melbourne. With this find the Director of Public Prosecutions said there was more than enough to convict them and send them all to prison for a good long time.

While the case against Jack for rape was not strong and they had decided not to proceed with this charge, they had an excellent case against him for being an accessory after the fact, and the Melbourne police had also found other pornographic images to investigate, which they had now linked indecent assault of other girls in that city.

It sounded simple but it had taken almost three years to put it all together. In the process they had gone to Broome and collected evidence from the school and other people in the community about the actions of the men there, testimony from the school principal about Dan's visit to Cathy, testimony from Alice about his visit to the restaurant, descriptions of all the men in Broome a week later. Then there was testimony of the mother and brother of Mimi in Newcastle and of the Alicia in Sydney along with that of others in the company office who provided more pieces of corroborating evidence.

Once the investigation had become known there had been endless obstruction and obfuscation, particularly after they seized the photos. She sensed that these men were running scared and were prepared to use every tactic, legal and illegal, to seek to escape the net. But now it had finally become a solid wall of evidence.

Nobody could foresee any problems and now the hearing was set to start on Monday for the first case, three charges of rape along with additional charges of carnal knowledge with persons under 16, against a Mr Martin Wallis.

Monday dawned bright and clear. A veritable army of lawyers and reporters was waiting outside the court before the doors opened. It was to be a preliminary stage this morning, presentation of initial arguments before a judge, then empanelling a jury.

Their barrister stood before the judge. He stated his case and laid out the charges.

Julie was curious how the other side would respond, the evidence seemed so clear to her. What she heard took her by surprise.

The defence barrister stood up and said. "Your honour, I move to have these charges dismissed. This is on the basis that this is a case of attempted entrapment by a person, Miss Julie McCredie, who has taken a personal dislike against the defendant and his friends.

Because of this she has gone about soliciting the assistance of others to fabricate evidence against Mr Wallis and his friends. None of these cases would have come to trial in this court if it was not for her actions in soliciting many persons of highly dubious character to come forward and fabricate evidence.

I wish to show to your honour a series of letters and documents including a letter from Miss McCredie asking her friend Lizzie Renford to make a statement against my client. I also tender two advertisements in the Sydney and Newcastle papers encouraging people who have been subject to sexual attacks or violence to come forward and provide Miss McCredie with information on their experiences. While there is not a mention of money Miss McCredie has also provided financial assistance to these witnesses as an incentive for them to make up these stories.

So your honour, I consider that the only way you can rule is that this is a case of purposeful entrapment where all the key witnesses for the prosecution have had their evidence solicited and even paid for by this vindictive woman.

It is well known that she is a crusader for women' rights and goes about seeking that charges be laid against those who she claims have had sex with non-consenting women despite all the evidence indicating that these women give themselves willingly. In this particular case this is shown clearly by these girls' sexual proclivities, including two having worked as prostitutes and the third having taken a large payment in return for sex.

On this basis I call for you to dismiss this case and also make a recommendation that the Director of Public Prosecution to also not proceed with charges against the other named parties.

Julie felt as if she had been struck by a rock in the head, nobody on her side had even considered this as an issue; surely it was not a basis on which the judge would have to do more than make a cursory rejection as yet another piece of avoidance.

She had heard a rumour that the judge had a family association with the Wallis family and in the past had been heard to comment that Martin was a fine young man. But surely this could not influence his decision as he sat on the bench and upheld the law of the land.

But now he was reading the submission handed to him closely and he looked like he was giving it serious thought. After a minute he announced that he needed to call an adjournment for an hour while he considered this request and looked up some matters of the law in this regard. They all filed out of court. She could see a gloating look on the face of Martin, as well as similar looks on the faces of Dan, Will and Jack who walked out alongside him.

Outside in the street she felt a buzz of excitement at this unexpected development. She knew that everyone was looking at her; it was all about her and the question of whether she had let her desire for vengeance lead her to gather evidence in some way that was not proper. Even though her mind said what she did was honourable, she had a sinking feeling.

An hour later all reconvened. Julie could feel her knees shaking.

Without any preliminaries the judge started speaking. It took a few seconds for Julie's mind to catch up with his words.

"I have considered the request of the defence. I rule in its favour. This case is dismissed. I also make a recommendation that the similar charges against the other two co-named defendants are withdrawn."

He then went on to make remarks about the prosecution's conduct of the case and Julie's role in soliciting evidence, but Julie was past hearing. All she could see was the gloating smirks of these four men as they walked from court, and much worse, in her mind were the hurt and desperate faces of these girls who had trusted her. She also felt she had failed all the thousands of other girls who had looked to them for courage.

Chapter 24 - Vindication

Yesterday had been a bitter disappointment to Julie, though Lizzie seemed to accept this as just a part of life's ups and downs. Julie's only consolation was a flood of support that had come from close friends and colleagues. There was also a well spring of public opinion in the editorials and letters against this decision.

The dismissal of the court case was something that really rankled with Julie, she had assembled her evidence through years of patient investigation, she had found a lawyer who believed in her and the justice of the cause, she had persuaded the public prosecutor to put together a brief of evidence against these three evil men, she had surmounted endless obstacles, threats and inertia to get the cases listed for trial, and to see these three men, along with their evil friend, standing in court. She knew they all needed to have their separate trials, the one who was charged with leading the offences and his two accomplices who faced similar charges, but were really just his patsies.

Then, to watch it all come unstuck in the first hour of the trial, really it was just the time for opening submissions, when the other side had used a technicality, which the judge had allowed, to rip their case apart.

The surprise from all in the court, particularly families and reporters, when this flimsy technicality was used to dismiss the case before any further consideration, ruling the whole basis of the charges as unsound, and determining that the defendant should be discharged, forthwith, no conviction recorded. Then, adding insult to injury, the judge had publicly censured the prosecution and her for bringing what he considered was an ill founded and ill prepared case.

It was front page headlines today, "Martin Wallis acquitted, judge dismisses case before any evidence is heard and censures prosecution for ill-founded, vindictive case." This lead article chose to cast no judgement on whether this decision was good or bad.

The paper also announced that the Director of Public Prosecutions had accepted the judge's recommendations and had withdrawn charges against the other named men in the related cases. So effectively all cases had been dismissed.

The rage was burning inside Julie now; she could taste that sour taste of failure, bitter in the back of her throat. It made her feel like gagging when she thought of these three horrible men, walking from the court with their glowing smirks, giving her an obscene sign, as they savoured their victory.

She had thought of staying in bed this morning, this loss had made her work seem so pointless, the bad guys always won. But, driven by her nascent rage, she had gone into the office, trying to maintain a brave defiance to this shambolic situation.

As she walked to her desk in the Sydney Morning Herald office she could almost sense the gloating of the women haters, those backward men in the office, the ones who had made so many 'behind the back' sneers, as the years had passed, whenever she had sought to pursue these issues. However she knew there was also strong support for her from others who worked away quietly at their own desks, both men and women; those young women who themselves had been threatened or worse by men like these, the fathers and mothers of daughters like Lizzie, Miranda and Alicia. She sensed a vast well of support against this judicial outrage and it roused her courage.

On her desk was a folded note. She picked it up absently, barely paying attention. It was from her editor, Michael Daly, who she knew was her staunch ally. "Please come to my office ASAP. Have been discussing with the MD and lawyers some options for not letting the bad guys win." Julie took a deep breath, she dared not hope, but could it be there was a way forward?

Michael was deep in conversation with two lawyers when she went in; Melissa their in-house counsel, and an older man she did not know personally, but recognised as a well respected Queens Counsel from her days in the courts. She stood and listened quietly.

Michael was speaking. "Well, if I understand you correctly it is not defamatory to print something that will be hugely offensive to the men concerned, provided it satisfies a public interest test and if it is also demonstrably true. And you are satisfied that the public interest test is easily met, now that the judge has dismissed the case and it is no longer before the court, and it is also demonstrably true as evidenced by the sworn affidavits of these three girls, particularly the testimony of Lizzie, including her age when her child was born."

The barrister was nodding his head. "Yes that is my advice." With that he packed up his papers and walked out the door, closely followed by the house counsel.

Michael waved Julie to a chair, then walked over, closed the door, and sat down alongside her. "I don't know how much you got of that, but this matter is far from finished, we might have lost in a court of law but now we can go to the court of public opinion and tell the full story that we could not tell before when they were facing charges.

"Now you need to write and we will print the story that lives in all those files. I was thinking of two articles, one which is a summary of the evidence against these three men which the jury never got to hear, because of the actions of the judge. The second, if your friend will agree to it, is the remarkable tale of that young woman, Lizzie, whose name I have read for months but who I have only had the pleasure to meet in the last few days.

I know you have already made a start on this, the rebuilding of the reputation of your friend. Who could ever forget that wonderful piece you wrote about her almost two years ago when you first made a part of her story known to the public. The response to that was huge. Now you must tell the full story, the parts you left out and of her continuing courage.

I never told you before, but many years ago I knew her father slightly, his father and mine were close friends. I would not live well with these two men's memories if I did not tell the daughters tale. She is a woman of rare bravery. Her story, more than anything, will bring justice, through the opinions and actions of that broad jury we call the peoples of this city, state and country.

They will now get to pass their own judgement. When it is done I think these men may well wish that they had instead stood before the judgement of the court. I have discussed this with the Managing Director of the paper. Despite being a naturally cautious man he has said he is with me all the way on this one. Plus he knows it will make great copy.

Julie returned to her desk and sat down to write the story.

Chapter 25- Lizzies Tale

Two days later, a large Sydney Morning Herald headline screamed out from the newsstands:

Child Rapist
Prominent business man Martin Wallis dodges Justice

Incontrovertible evidence of their role in the rape of two fourteen year old girls and one fifteen year old girls in Sydney over the last ten years ago never made it to court three days ago. Mr Martin Wallis and two other prominent Sydney businessmen used a legal technicality to avoid facing charges of rape in the Sydney Supreme Court on Monday this week. Now it is up to this paper to seek right for these victims.

As reported in this paper the judge used a legal technicality to dismiss charges against three men, Mr Martin Wallis, Mr Daniel Ashcroft and Mr William Brown, determining that almost all the evidence was inadmissible and therefore the case would not proceed to trial.

This decision has defeated the hope of justice for these three girls, despite each being brutally raped, in a pre-planned and calculated matter by these three men. This denial of justice has occurred despite sworn statements clearly identifying these men and telling of their actions, both by these girls and by many other witnesses who have corroborated these events. There is also clear photographic evidence of these men's crimes.

Previously the Herald has not been able to publish these details due to the cases being before Court. However now all these cases have been dismissed the Herald is free to publish the results of its own investigations into the actions of these three vile and cowardly men. It encourages these men to sue it for defamation if they consider they have grounds. It would look forward to this evidence being tested in court should this arise.

In the meantime this publication is the only way the Herald sees for a measure of recompense to be given to these three brave girls who, despite many threats and intimidation, have each come forward to tell their stories.

For those of you, our readers, who feel the same level of outrage we do, please make these sentiments known to your local elected representatives. Demand they fix this legal nonsense.

Based on this travesty of a legal decision the Herald calls on the Attorney General to investigate laying new charges against these men.

It also calls on the publicly listed company Newcastle Transport, for which Mr Martin Wallis is Executive Director, to take prompt action to terminate his appointment in this role, as one unfit for such a responsible position.

For full story see Page 3. For the story of one of these incredibly courageous girls, and how she had rebuilt her life after this awful event see 'Lizzie's Tale' on Page 5. This gives the true and full story of the school friend of our investigative reporter, Julie McCredie, which was featured two years ago as "Sophie's Story" to huge public interest. You may feel you already know the tale of this remarkable woman, now read how it really happened.

Some readers turned to page three and read the lurid details. Most turned to page five and read Lizzie's Tale. Many could be seen sitting on park benches, with the newspapers open on their laps, some with tears running down their cheeks.

Lizzies Tale – Story by Julie McCredie

I tell this story of my friend, Lizzie and how I betrayed her, to my ongoing shame. Lizzie was the brightest girl in my class and my best friend at Balmain High School in 1963. We did our intermediate certificate together and she was dux of the year. She had her life before her and her future was bright even though her family was poor, just a mother and a small brother. Her father died in an accident over six years earlier. Now, to help her mother pay the bills, she worked all her free time, ironing, baby-sitting, doing laundry; anything that paid a little money. She had little time to study but she still got top marks.

On the Saturday after the school year finished I went to her fifteenth birthday party. She was so proud and happy, her mother had scrimped and saved everything she owned to buy Lizzie a beautiful dress; a dress her Dad would have been proud to see Lizzie wearing.

At this party I introduced Lizzie to my friend Carl Richards. Through him she was introduced Martin Wallis and his two friends, Dan and Will. I did not really like or trust them but I never tried to warn or protect Lizzie from them, she was just a naïve and trusting teenager. She had barely met any boys before as she had been so busy working.

They invited her to come to a party the next weekend. As I wanted to go with Carl and needed Lizzie to help me trick my parents into letting me go, I encouraged her to come too. On the way to the party, Martin took us to a hotel in Darlinghurst. There he plied Lizzie with glasses of sherry. Lizzie had never tried sherry before. I could see she was getting drunk.

Then at the party I went off with Carl and left Lizzie with these three men. They continued to give her champagne to drink. I could see she was getting really tipsy and unsteady on her feet, but I did not try to look after her. Later I looked for her but she had disappeared, along with Martin and his friends.

An hour later Martin was back but there was no Lizzie, he said Lizzie had gone home sick, catching the bus. He had a funny grin on his face, as did his friends, like they seemed really pleased with something they had done.

Next day I went to Lizzie's house to see how she was. She did not want to see me but when her mother let me in she was lying on her bed, crying and crying. She told me to go away, she would not tell me what had happened and I did not really try to find out.

Lizzie dropped out of school, stopped seeing her friends, got a job at a factory. No one could understand what had happened to this beautiful and happy girl, we forgot about her.

The next time I saw Lizzie was seven months later. One winter's day Lizzie came to see me at boarding school. She said she wanted to say goodbye and was sorry for being awful to me, she was going to Melbourne to live, just by herself. She had saved seventy pounds at the factory. Lizzie was now seven months pregnant. She asked me to tell her mother. She was determined to have the baby. She knew if she stayed in Sydney she would be forced to give up her baby for adoption.

I made Lizzie tell me what had happened on that night and she did.

When Lizzie was getting really drunk and needed to sit down, Martin walked her out to his car and got her to sit in the back seat. He sat next to her, putting his arm around her so she could not get out.

Then despite her protests Will and Dan got into the car as well. They took her to the beach at Nielsen Park, just her with three strong men.

They said, "You didn't think we brought a pretty little poor girl out to a party just to admire her did you. Now it is time to pay us back for being nice to you."

Then two of them held her down while the third one raped her and each took their turn. When they were finished they said she would be stupid to tell anyone, because no one would believe her.

In shame and terror Lizzie ran off and finally found her way back to her home next day while her mother was at church. She would tell no one. We, her friends, made little effort to find out and help. Two months later Lizzie discovered she was going to have a baby from that awful night, her only time with a man; she had never even held hands with or kissed a boy before.

She did not know what to do and at first tried to pretend it was not true. Then she felt the baby move and knew she wanted to have it, she decided that she would love this child despite its awful conception. She knew that if the secret came out it would be taken from her and she was determined not to let this happen. So she hid her pregnancy and saved her money.

At the same time she made a plan that when her secret was found out she would catch a train to Melbourne and have her baby there and find a way to keep it. On this day, when I saw her again, the factory where she worked, had just discovered her pregnancy and sacked her.

Now this fifteen year old girl, with only seventy pounds, was going to a city where she knew no one, so she could keep her baby, a baby that was the result of that rape by these brutal men.

When I found this out I was so ashamed at my part. But Lizzie said to me, "Don't feel bad, you could not have known what would happen. And despite the awful way in which it happened, this baby is something to be loved and cherished."

Next time I heard from Lizzie was a few months later. She was in Perth waiting for the boat to take her to Broome. She had her baby, Catherine, now just ten weeks old with her. At first Lizzie had tried to support herself by working in a café, but when she was down to her last ten pounds she had taken a job as a prostitute.

She said it was simple; her only choice was to do this so as to be able to keep and feed her baby. There was no self-pity; in fact she was proud and in control of her life. She had now saved three hundred pounds. Then someone had found out about her age, still not sixteen, and the baby. They told the authorities and she knew they were searching for her. She realised she must leave Melbourne that afternoon or Social Security and the Police would come and take her baby away and place her in a remand home. So she caught a train to Adelaide and then Perth. She was still running.

So she went to the farthest side of the country, just her and her tiny baby to start a new life again. The letter said not to worry about her, her life had been hard when first she came to Melbourne, but now she was rich and going to a new place, where no one would find here. Here she knew she could make a new life for herself with the money she had saved.

The next time I heard from Lizzie was over two years later. She was now eighteen. She owned her own café in Broome, and had two thousand pounds in the bank. She sent me a photo of her and second photo of Catherine, playing with other children in the street. They both looked beautiful and so happy.

For Lizzie all those bad things were a distant memory and she looked forward to seeing me again one day, she said in another year or two if her business kept growing she would fly to Sydney with her baby to see her Mum and she would visit me too.

She said she had left her life as a street girl in Melbourne behind, as she did not want her child to grow up with that, even though she had no personal shame. It was a necessity that life had forced on her, but she would prefer that her daughter and mother did not know.

The years went by and for a while I heard no more from Lizzie. Finally I heard from Lizzie again three years ago, another letter which told me the last part of this tale. One of the men who had raped her had discovered she was living in Broome. Now he came to see her.

He told her that the three men who had raped her before, along with another man who had tried to abuse her in Melbourne, were all coming to Broome in a week's time. They all knew she was there and they expected to spend a night with her, "to repeat their former pleasures," he said. If she did not give them what they wanted they would tell the whole town of her life as a prostitute. They also threatened harm to her daughter.

Lizzie was terrified; she did not know what to do, she was in fear for her daughter, in fear for herself. Perhaps she should have fought back, asked her friends for help, gone to the police. But these were powerful and wealthy men; it was her word against four of them.

She took the only choice she could see, she ran again. This time she took her car, her six year old daughter and a handful of possessions. She was almost totally unprepared but set out to drive across the desert to Alice Springs. Somehow, in her panicked brain, she felt that safety lay with distance and she must keep running, putting distance between herself and these evil men.

A hundred miles into the desert Lizzie's car broke down, leaving her and her daughter with almost no water or food, in a barren and pitiless landscape. Almost certainly she would have died, had it not been for a couple strange, almost miraculous, coincidences.

One was a friend of her childhood, Sophie, from back when she was eight years old and lived in their house in Balmain. Sophie came to her daughter, Catherine, appearing in her mind. She told her the way to a small pool of water, hidden a mile out in the desert. This water kept them alive when they otherwise would have died of thirst.

Three days later they were rescued by a group of aborigines who took then to their own place in the desert. These people fed them, they shared their houses. They hugged and played with Catherine, they made Lizzie into one of their family.

So Lizzie now lives in the desert with a small aboriginal tribe. Since going there she has married her true love. They now have two more children. She and her husband Robbie are the happiest people I know.

They share all they have with these aboriginal people and these people share all they have in return. Lizzie teaches all the children to read and write, Robbie helps with building and fixing things, the people share their knowledge of the desert and share their desert food, they teach her children the aboriginal ways and stories.

When I asked Lizzie to help me pursue and bring to justice these evil men, those who raped her when she was fifteen and fathered her first child, she agreed to do so. But she told me it was not in retribution for herself; she needs nothing from them and nothing they or anyone else can say can touch her happiness anymore.

But she said she needed to do it to stop them from hurting others, Mimi and Alicia and the many others whose names we do not know but who are out there too. Lizzie was not the first person they raped, and there have been many others since. We only know of three so far, but we know there will be others who hide the same secret.

So Lizzie says to them all, to Mimi and Alicia who she has met and hugged and cried with, and to the others to whom she would give her love if she knew your names.

"Have courage, speak out, tell your story! Do not let them make you run and hide like I did."

And to us all she says; "Do not allow this outrage to go on. Do not allow these men to hide from their crimes through a legal fiction. Demand justice for them all. Speak!

This paper says too. Take up the cause of this injustice. It could have been your daughter or your sister who suffered this. Do not let these awful men get away with their outrageous behaviour, Act now. Make sure it never happens to another girl like Lizzie again!

Chapter 26 - Return to the Desert

The day the paper published the story all the phones rang of their hooks, both at the newspaper and at the offices of every politician. Most were women though some men rang through to lend support too, and a few brave or stupid men tried to defend the indefensible.

But how could anyone say that it was anything but criminal for these three men to have deliberately plotted to rape fourteen and fifteen year old girls and to have continued this behaviour many times over at least ten years.

Lizzie's was the first testimony but it was generally agreed that she was by no means their first victim; all were agreed that her testimony suggested prior events and a practised method. Then there was a known second case three years later and the last case, they knew of, barely two years ago, in this case involving a fourth man.

It enraged the public beyond belief that they had been denied the opportunity to see the men face trial by a legal technicality. By the end of the day a trading halt had been called on the shares on Newcastle Transport, with a fall of over 50% percent in the listed share price. With the expansion that the firm had done over the last two years, the share holding of Mr Martin Wallis was now reduced to less than 35%. So, with the desertion of support from all the other board members, his position was untenable along with that of his three friends. By the end of the day all had lost their jobs.

The general business opinion was that nothing could save the company now, it was over geared and its business revenues would collapse due to the level of outrage across wide sections of the community, leading to demands that no future contracts with this firm be entered into. There was a wide view that all shares in the company would be worthless by the end of the month and, as soon as trading resumed, a fire-sale was expected.

From the accused men the silence was deafening. They had all gone to ground, no one could find them. Despite journalists searching high and low there was nothing to indicate where they had gone. Not that this was any surprise, the public felt they knew the real measure of their characters, the word despicable was widely used.

There were suggestions of a new trial being launched. The DPP had given an undertaking to review all evidence again to see if new grounds or offences could be found for a further trial. In addition several further girls and women had come forward claiming a similar experience and there was widespread opinion that this would give the basis for further charges. Commentators speculated on civil damages claims being launched by the injured parties as well. It was considered likely these would bankrupt the three individuals and perhaps affect the company further.

All this largely passed Robbie and Lizzie by. They politely declined requests for interviews. Their representatives merely re-iterated that they stood by their stories and they would leave it for others to discuss what may follow.

Lizzie spent time with her mother, brother and close friends when not with Robbie or her children. Robbie swam in the harbour and walked along the Balmain streets relying on his largely unknown status to keep his freedom from being drawn in.

But the journalists were now beginning to hound the family, to stop outside the Balmain house in the hope for doorstop interviews, to try and snap photos of the children at play, or Lizzie through the window. Lizzie was pleased that justice had been served in this strange public way, but she had no desire to continue her celebrity status.

After four days, Robbie came home from a walk and said that today some people had connected him with the case and had taken to following him with cameras and trying to ask questions. He was polite and thanked them for their well-meaning concern. But it was all becoming a complete pain in the behind.

So they made a mutual decision that enough was enough, they would take the flight tomorrow which returned to Darwin and the connecting flight to Broome the following morning.

It left early in the morning. Before the journalists woke up they were gone in a taxi to the airport. The next day they came back to Broome, on a steamy hot day, feeling pleasure in freedom.

But even here some assiduous journalists followed. So they packed up their bus, a four wheel drive camper model, and drove to the desert, down past Halls Creek.

It was late in the evening when they came to this place, the place which Cathy called Sophie's Place, on the rock ridge gazing out across endless desert dunes. The stars were out. A low half-moon hung in the mid-sky. The five of them stood together gazing in awe at the bright desert sky. This was their place; the desert had brought them home and now welcomed them back into its endless embrace.

About the Author

Graham Wilson lives in Sydney Australia. He has completed and published nine books, including three in this Old Balmain House Series.

His first novel in this series, tells the story of a small girl who went missing 100 years ago with her best friend and was never found, leaving a trail of grief down through generations until the finally her story is discovered. It is based in the real Balmain, an early inner Sydney suburb, with its real locations and historical events providing part of the story background. This second novel in this series, 'Lizzie's Tale' builds on "The Old Balmain House" setting, It is the story of a working class teenage girl who lives in this same house in the 1950s and 1960s, It tells of how she becomes pregnant she is determined not to surrender her baby for adoption, and her struggle to survive. The series concludes with the book 'Devils Choice' which follows the life of Lizzie's daughter Catherine and the awful choice she too must make through confronting her mother's rapists.

Graham has also written five novels in the Crocodile Spirit Dreaming Series. The first novel 'An English Visitor' tells the story of an English backpacker, Susan, who visits the Northern Territory and becomes captivated and in great danger from a man who loves crocodiles. The second book in the series, 'Creature of an Ancient Dreaming', follows the consequences of the first book based around the discovery of this man's remains and the main character being placed on trial for murder. The third book, 'The Empty Place', is about the struggle of the main character to retain her sanity in jail while her family and friends desperately try to find out what really happened on that fateful day before it is too late. Book 4, 'Lost Girls' is the story of four missing backpackers whose lives are revealed in this man's diary. It is also the story of the search for the main character who has vanished too. Book 5, 'Sunlit Shadow Dance' concludes the series and begins with a girl who appears in a remote aboriginal community with no memory and how she rebuilds her life but alongside this come dark shadows that threaten to overwhelm her.

Graham has also written a family memoir "Children of Arnhem's Kaleidoscope." It tells of his childhood in an aboriginal community in remote Arnhem Land, in Australia's Northern Territory, one of its last frontiers. It tells of the people, danger and beauty of this place, and of its transformation over the last half century with the coming of aboriginal rights and the discovery or uranium. It also tells of his surviving an attack by a large crocodile.

In his non writing life he is a veterinarian who has worked with zoo animals, on large cattle stations and in national parks.

More information about Graham and his books and writing is available from the following sites:

Graham Wilson – Australian Author on Facebook
Graham Wilson Author Profile on Smashwords and Amazon
Graham Wilson's Publishing Web Page
        www.beyondbeyondbooks.com.au

If you want to contact Graham directly please use the email:
        grahambbbooks@gmail.com